Loving a Landon

The Barrington Billionaires
Book Eleven

Ruth Cardello

Author Contact
website: RuthCardello.com
email: ruthcardello@gmail.com
Facebook: Author Ruth Cardello
Twitter: RuthieCardello
Goodreads
goodreads.com/author/show/4820876.Ruth_Cardello
Bookbub
bookbub.com/authors/ruth-cardello

Copyright

Print Edition

ISBN eBook: 978-1-951888-20-6
ISBN Print: 978-1-951888-21-3

An original work of Ruth Cardello, 2021.

Loving a Landon

Benjamin Drover thought he'd found love until his wife joined the Marines and was killed in action. He's spent the last year, hating everyone—including himself. On the anniversary of his wife's death, he receives a letter from her, asking him to donate her entire inheritance to the Landon Foundation.

He's angry with her for leaving, angry with himself for not moving on, and driven beyond fury when the always irreverent Clay Landon refuses the donation.

Born to one of the world's wealthiest families, Clay's sister, Caterina, has had anything but an easy life. After losing her parents and one of her older brothers, the ultimate betrayal came from Clay himself. What he did to her, how she suffered because of him, was something she is still recovering from. She doesn't regret walking away from her inheritance, but she is tired of the past controlling her. It's time to face it, face Clay, and finally begin to heal.

Her whole life is upside-down. It's definitely the wrong time to meet the right man.

Caterina's pain tears through Benjamin's anger. He wants to help her, but first, he must heal his own wounds. To keep her, he'll need to become the man he always should have been.

This time, when the woman he loves announces she's

going to battle—he'll go with her.

And if Clay Landon survives, he just might get to play Fairy Godfather one more time.

Dedication

This book is dedicated to my friend Caterina.
Thank you for always being a ray of sunshine in my day and
for lending me your name for this book.

Chapter One

Benjamin

I'M HERE TO see Clay Landon," I said to a receptionist behind a tall glass semicircle of a desk. The sign behind her read The Landon Foundation. The heart of Boston's business district was an expensive location for a nonprofit, but Clay Landon was said to be one of the richest men in the world. His true net worth was unknown and spread around the globe. He was also nearly impossible to pin down for a meeting.

"Do you have an appointment?" she inquired with a pleasant enough smile.

"I do. Benjamin Drover." I didn't smile back. I'd stopped being pleasant the day a Marine Corps officer and Navy chaplain had shown up at my house to inform me that Tasha would not be returning home.

"Please have a seat. Mr. Landon should be here any moment."

Irritated, I rose to my full height. "He's not here?" Very few things lured me out of my office lately. The Landon Foundation didn't accept large donations without the donor meeting with Clay Landon in person—and on his turf.

The receptionist's smile remained bright. "He will be shortly. He's aware of his appointment with you. If you'd like to take a seat, I could bring you a coffee or a water."

"He has five minutes." If I hadn't been there to fulfill a written wish from Tasha I would have given the receptionist quite a different message to pass along. I was trapped—guilt proving a stronger tether than any material could.

A year without her should have been enough to free me, but it had done the opposite. Had Tasha lived, there was a good chance we wouldn't have stayed together. Or maybe we would have. I'd never know.

A few days earlier, on the anniversary of her death, her lawyer had delivered a letter to me from her. It hadn't said she loved me. Looking back, I was sure we didn't share the same definition of love anyway.

Tasha had lived and died on her own terms. Every move she'd made had been part of a larger plan. She won by doing so much for people that when she asked them for something, they felt they had very little choice but to agree to her terms.

Beautiful. Intelligent. Cunning. I'd been no match for her when she decided to make me part of her plans. Her parents had wanted her to get a college degree so she had. They'd wanted her to marry into a good family—that's where I'd come in.

I wouldn't have married her had I understood that nothing I wanted figured into her plans. She took my name, played the role of a happy wife for a few months, then dropped the bomb that she'd enlisted in the Marines.

Not that she'd wanted to enlist. No, by the time she'd told me, she'd signed the paperwork and it was a done deal. She didn't just want to serve, she wanted to be a Recon officer. Impossible? Not according to her.

At first, I was in shock. It had to be a phase.

Then I got angry. All the promises she'd made me had been lies.

Once, drunk, I'd begged her to come home.

I went through a dark period where every day it felt like I was simply going through the motions of living.

Then I got angry again.

And drunk a time or two more.

I was ready to tell her we were over, but I wasn't ready to hear she was gone.

A year on my own had given me time and distance from the loss of her, but the pain had returned in full force as I'd read her letter. In the event of her death, in celebration of the anniversary of it, she wanted the entirety of her trust fund to be donated to the Landon Foundation.

In celebration? There was nothing about our time together that put me in the mood to celebrate. And why me? She could have requested her parents arrange it. In her letter, she said she'd chosen me because she'd known I was strong enough to survive her.

She said she'd always known I would be the one to fulfill her final wish. Why? Why me? The question haunted me.

"I'll tell Mr. Landon you're waiting." The woman ducked down to send a message. "Please have a seat."

I stepped away, but remained standing. *Fucking Landon.*

This didn't have to be complicated. The sooner he showed up and accepted the donation from me, the sooner I could move on.

Four minutes. Five. Eight.

Clay Landon strolled up to the receptionist and began chatting with her like he had nowhere to go and no one waiting for him. By the time he turned and scanned the area, I was furious.

"Ben," Landon called with a wave. "Come into my office."

"Benjamin," I corrected as I walked toward him. "Benjamin Drover."

"So serious. Welcome Benjamin Drover. I'm Clay Landon."

I know who you fucking are. Let's get this over with. I thought it, but didn't say it. I would have, but he wasn't worth the time an argument would take.

"I hope you weren't waiting long," Clay added.

I didn't bother to respond. He didn't care. I followed Clay into a relatively empty office. No books. No computer. The only thing on his desk was a photo of a blonde woman.

Clay waved to the chairs in front of his desk. "Have a seat."

"This won't take that long," I said. "I'm here to make a donation to the Landon Foundation for the Gold Star Initiative."

Clay paced back and forth. "What's your opinion on family?"

"Excuse me?"

"And respecting boundaries. I should be able to tell people that my relationship or lack of one with my family is none of their business and they should respect that, correct?"

"I'd rather stick to the reason I'm here."

"Sure. Sure. Sorry, I just had lunch with my friends and I'm frustrated. They want to know about my family. I told them I don't have any. Okay, I'd admitted to one cousin, but the rest are dead to me."

I gave Clay a look that I hoped expressed how little interest I had in the topic.

Clay continued, "My wife's memory is too good. I may have once told her I had siblings. She accused me of lying because since then she's heard me say I don't. I don't consider choosing a reality I can live with and maintaining it lying."

"That's the definition of lying."

"Is it? It shouldn't be. Lying implies the truth is someone else's business and, in my opinion, in this case, it isn't."

That struck a nerve in me. "Doesn't sound like you have a very good marriage. She deserves better."

"We have a great marriage." Clay rose to his feet. "This isn't about that, it's about me."

"Well, that's a selfish version of love." It all sounded too familiar for me to be able to stomach it. "Don't bother to consider how what you do might affect your spouse."

Sinking into his seat, Clay said, "Selfish? I am always looking for ways to help other people." His eyes narrowed. "My relationship with any family I may or may not have shouldn't affect anyone but myself."

"I have twenty million dollars I would like to donate to your foundation today. Is it possible for us to discuss that?" I checked my watch. "I need to make some calls before the offices in London close for the day."

Clay tilted his head to the side. "You work?" he asked with awed sympathy as if I'd admitted to panhandling.

"Of course."

"Twenty million is a lot of money." He tapped a hand on the arm of his chair. "And I've never heard of you."

I took a deep breath. "I'll have the funds released to your foundation later today. Thank you for your time."

Clay jumped to his feet. "Wait, I haven't agreed to accept it."

What? "Are you saying you don't want the donation?"

"No need to get all upset. There's a vetting process. I can't accept money from everyone who wants to give some to me, especially sizable contributions. I need to know more about you before your name is linked to the foundation."

"It can be anonymous for all I care." My irritation grew.

"That tone." Clay let out a whistle. "If you want to donate to the Landon Foundation you'll have to bring a better attitude to the table." He waved a hand toward the open door. "Do you even know what we do?"

"At this office? It's your Gold Star Initiative. You support the families of fallen soldiers. It's a worthwhile program and the only reason I'm still standing here."

"I don't believe you." He gave me a long look. "What am I missing? You came to me, I didn't seek you out. Why all the anger?"

"I'm not angry." I ground the words out between clenched teeth.

He rubbed a hand over his chin. "That's what Lexi says right before she tells me why she is. People should just say how they feel. Own it. I'll start. I feel horrible that I lied to my wife and friends. I do have relatives who are still alive and breathing, but I don't want anything to do with them. I don't want to talk to them. I don't want to even think about them. Why should I have to?"

Losing what little was left of my patience, I snapped, "Because you're not a child and it's not all about you. Do you honestly believe I'd still be talking to you if I had another option?"

"Well, that's rude. And I was about to ask you if you wanted to go somewhere for coffee. I've given up drinking and some days it is not easy."

"If I walk out of here you won't hear from me again. Are you okay with your foundation missing out on something this big?"

"I am, but I'm curious why you appear not to be. What would you do if I said I don't want your money?"

I threw up both hands. "I'm done. I can't do this. Sorry, Tasha. You should have chosen a charity run by someone who isn't completely insane."

"Who's Tasha?"

Emotions running high, I growled out, "Someone who believed in your cause. She was a Marine, a hero, and my wife."

"Was?"

"She was killed in action, saving civilians."

"I'm sorry." A heavy silence hung in the room. "She sent you here?"

Just how slow is he? "Yes. She specifically asked for her estate to be donated to your Gold Star Initiative."

"I understand now. She knew you'd need us."

"I don't need anyone."

"I used to think that, then I met my best friend, Dax. He introduced me to the Barringtons. Through them I met my wife, Lexi. My life is now ripe with people I can't imagine it without. More recently I've successfully played the role of Fairy Godfather Extraordinaire. Sadly, all that good left people with an expectation that I'm perfect. I'm not. Jacqueline understands that. It's why she never brought up our family with Lexi. Jacqueline is my cousin. She knows how messed up my family is."

"Is there anyone else in the office who could take a check from me today?"

"Normally I'd direct you to Connor Sutton. However, he and his wife are on holiday after finishing filming his latest movie. I'll make a deal with you. I'll accept your donation if you agree to attend one surviving spouse support group meeting."

"No deal," Benjamin answered automatically. The last thing I needed was to sit around and listen to people talk about how they were struggling after a loss. I wasn't struggling. In fact, as soon as this final task was completed all I expected to feel was free. "Do you want the money or not?"

Clay folded his arms across his chest. "One meeting."

"Not going to happen." This was bordering on ridiculous. I expected him to cave as I increased the pressure. "Last chance to accept."

Lowering his arms, Clay smiled. "Have a nice day, Mr. Drover. I'm sure I'll see you again."

"I'm sure you won't." With that I strode out of Clay's office. As I made my way toward the elevator I cursed beneath my breath. As Clay had said, twenty million was a lot of money. Did it really belong in the hands of someone who was clearly unstable? Surely there were other charities, better ones with more accountability. I would contact Tasha's lawyer and ask if there was a contingency plan.

I was still deep in thought when the elevator door opened and I stepped inside, not noticing a petite woman until we crashed into each other. She stumbled backward and fell against the back wall.

"Oh, shit," I said, rushing forward. "I didn't see you. Are you okay?"

"Sorry, I wasn't paying attention." The woman brought a hand to the back of her head. "I'm fine. Just a little bump."

"Let me help you up." I held out a hand to her. She took it and I easily hauled her to her feet. Upright she only came to mid chest on me. Our eyes met and for a moment there was nothing else but her and those beautiful eyes of hers. Long curls framed her face. No makeup. She didn't need any. Although she was dressed in simple slacks and a modest short-sleeved blouse, she packed quite a sexual punch. On any other day I would have asked for her number, but I was in a foul mood.

The elevator door closed and she said, "Oh, no, that was my floor."

I turned to scan the lit numbers on the panel and realized I was still holding her hand. I let it drop. "Looks like you might need to go down to go back up."

Her cheeks flushed and she looked away. "Looks that way. I hope this isn't a sign I shouldn't be here."

A surge of protectiveness swept through me. I hadn't felt anything for anyone for so long I didn't like it. I kept my tone even. "I don't believe in signs."

"You're right." She nodded and sniffed. "I didn't come this far to lose courage now."

Courage? That didn't sound good. When the elevator reached the bottom floor the door opened, but I didn't get out. I told myself to, but my feet stayed planted where they were. "Are you applying for a job?"

She pressed the button for the floor we'd just come from. "No." She squared her shoulders and raised her chin then smoothed her hands down the sides of her slacks. "I'm here to see someone I never thought I'd want to again."

"Who?" The question had been uncontainable.

She pressed her lips in a straight line before answering. "My brother Clay. We haven't seen each other in over ten years." She flashed an overly bright smile and held up crossed fingers. "Wish me luck."

"Good luck."

It could be a different Clay. And even if it isn't, it's none of my business. I refuse to care about this.

Clay Landon is batshit crazy and there are hundreds of

women who would be a whole lot less complicated to fuck.

I'm not doing this.

The elevator door opened and she disappeared through it. I rode down to the lobby then made my way to the parking garage. I didn't allow myself to think about much until I was behind the wheel of my car.

Instead of starting the engine, I sat there. Ten years was a long time to not speak to someone. What could have happened between them? Whatever it was, Clay was far from over it. That was one meeting that wasn't going to go well.

There's nothing I can do.

I don't know her.

I don't want to know Clay.

I should drive away and forget about both of them.

Chapter Two

Caterina

I STOPPED IN the hallway that led to my brother's office and slumped against the wall. I wanted to chase after Mr. Gorgeous-eyes and beg him to stay, but I didn't.

No. I can do this on my own.

I'm a survivor. Strong. Independent. Fearless.

There'd been years when I'd prayed for someone to rescue me. No one had. Even my younger brother, Cooper, had withdrawn to face his own demons.

No turning back now. I should have done this a long time ago. I slapped myself lightly on both cheeks. Focus.

Straightening off the wall, I adjusted the hem of my blouse. It won't be easy. Family never is. I opened a glass door and made my way to the reception desk. Forcing a bright smile, I said, "Hello. I'm here to see Clay Landon."

The woman looked down at her desk then shook her head. "I'm sorry, Mr. Landon isn't seeing anyone else today."

"But he is here?"

The woman blinked quickly. "Mr. Landon doesn't see anyone without an appointment."

"He'll see me." I hiked my purse higher on my shoulder. "I'm his sister."

The woman's eyes narrowed. "As I said Mr. Landon doesn't see anyone without an appointment."

In all the scenarios that had played out in my imagination, I hadn't considered that he would flat-out refuse to see me. "Tell him I'm here." If he didn't want anything to do with me, I needed to hear it from him.

The receptionist folded her hands on the desk in front of her. "I'm sorry, I can't do that. He told me he doesn't want to be disturbed." Looking me directly in the eye, she added, "If you are his sister, though, you're welcome to call him and perhaps he'll come out to meet you."

It wasn't easy to admit, but I said, "I don't have his number."

"Of course."

God, she was smug. Rather than reaching across the desk and giving the receptionist the smack she was begging for, I dug through my purse until I found my wallet then pulled out my license and held it up. "Caterina Landon."

The woman's shoulders rose and lowered. "Impressive, but my cousin made me a fake ID when I was underage. He was twelve." She pressed a button, leaned forward and said, "Could you please come out to the reception area?"

Thank God. I guess I wore her down. Relief flooded through me even as I once again became anxious. "Thank you for believing me."

The woman nodded.

When a door opened, I held my breath. I didn't believe

in pouring energy into negative experiences, but there was no moving forward until I faced the past. I had questions only Clay could answer.

It took me a moment to accept that the man walking toward me was not my brother but a security guard. When the truth slammed in, my anxiety fell away, replaced by anger.

"Please come with me," the security guard said.

I held my license up for him to see as well. "I am not leaving without talking to my brother. My name is Caterina Landon."

The security guard looked at the receptionist who shook her head and said, "Mr. Landon doesn't have any siblings. He told me so himself when my brother came for a visit."

That rocked me back onto my heels. I slowly put my license back in my wallet. My voice was hoarse when I asked, "He said that?"

I'd always known Clay didn't care about me. He'd changed after our parents had died. But to deny that I existed? That was a new low even for Clay.

The security guard appeared conflicted when he met my gaze again. "I've heard a lot of creative stories from people trying to get in to meet Mr. Landon, but being his sibling is a first. Do you have anything that could prove who you are other than that ID? A photo of you together?"

Yeah, no. "Nothing on my phone and nothing recent."

"I'm sorry." The man raised a hand to point to the exit. "I'll escort you out."

There has to be something I can say. I hadn't come to

Boston to leave without saying my piece. "If Clay doesn't actually have a sister then what's the harm of at least mentioning my name to him?"

The guard shifted from one foot to another. "I guess not much."

"Much less than discovering you turned away his family."

"Family he says he doesn't have."

"My brother has always been a very private man. He protects us by keeping us a secret." It was a blatant lie. Clay had never lifted a finger to protect me or Cooper, but the truth wouldn't help me see him. "He won't be happy to hear he missed my visit."

The guard took out his phone. "I'll mention your name, but that's it."

I linked my hands in front of me and waited while the guard sent a text. A moment later a door opened and I swayed on my feet as Clay walked through it.

"Caterina?" He looked as shaken as I felt.

"Mr. Landon," the receptionist said in a rush, "I—" He waved her off and continued to walk toward me.

I dropped my hands, squared my shoulders, and looked him in the eye. "So inconvenient when someone you told people doesn't exist appears, isn't it?"

To the guard, Clay said, "You can go." He cleared his throat. "Why don't we step into my office. . ."

"Yes," I bit out, "I'm sure that would be best."

He gave me a long look as we walked. "It is you."

I followed him into his office then stood even after he

offered me a seat. We stared at each other until I couldn't take it anymore. "You don't have to worry, I'm not here for money. I don't care what you did with my share of our inheritance."

"All your money is still there—if you finally want it."

"Sure it is. You don't need to lie to me. I already said that's not why I'm here."

"Then why are you here?"

This was it. I'd finally get the answer to a question I'd asked myself a million times. "I need to know why—what did Cooper and I do to you that we deserved what happened to us? Yes, I was with Collin the night he died. Do you think I haven't tortured myself about that? We were young and stupid. But why punish Cooper too? He was fourteen and not even at the party."

"I never punished anyone."

I laughed without humor. "I know it was your idea. Did you hope we'd die there? Make it even easier for you to take our money? We didn't. We survived. Healed. We went on without you."

"Healed? From what? What are you talking about?"

"Don't you dare pretend you don't know. I know exactly how involved you were."

"Listen, you can think whatever you want, but you're the one who said everything was my fault. That was right before you said it would have been better for everyone if I'd been the one who died instead of Collin. Oh, yes, and then warned you'd take out a restraining order on me if I ever contacted you again."

"Could you blame me? After what you did?" I shuddered and hugged my purse to me. I wasn't a violent person, but I was tempted to be. How could he look at me and lie so easily? "You are exactly why I know I'm better off without my inheritance. Look at what money did to you. I'm not sorry for anything I said. I'm so sick of seeing your face in the news when you win another humanitarian award. There is nothing human about you."

After a heavy moment of silence, Clay asked, "Why are you attacking me? I didn't do anything."

"Oh, that's how you want to play it? You're rewriting history to fit your new image? I guess I would too, if I were you. The Barringtons wouldn't want anything to do with you if they knew the truth."

"You're not making any sense. Just what is it you think I did?"

I was so angry I was shaking. "I didn't expect you to apologize, but I thought you would at least pretend to be sorry." I turned and flung the door open. "But like always, regardless of how little I ask of you, it's still too much."

"Caterina—wait." Clay was at the door before I had time to step through it.

I shook my head. Disgust brought bile up my throat. "I came for closure and I have it. I always wondered if I made the right choice. I did. I can move on now. So, thanks for that."

"Don't go."

My emotions were riding too high to care that he finally sounded sad. "There's nothing to stay for. Goodbye, Clay.

You may now resume pretending I don't exist."

He said something else, but I didn't stop to listen. I bolted out of his office and past the receptionist's desk. It wasn't my proudest moment. It was also a much shorter meeting than I'd imagined it would be. Still, I'd stayed for all I could handle.

Rather than waiting for the elevator, I sprinted down the stairs. I don't know how many floors I'd gone down before I realized I hadn't thought that decision through. Fifty stories? My legs were exhausted by the time I reached the lobby. I stopped just outside the stairway door and covered my eyes with my hands.

No more wondering what it would be like if I ran into Clay somewhere. No more second-guessing myself about if I should have cut him out of my life. I'm finally free.

I didn't feel free, though. I felt very, very alone.

And sad.

"Are you okay?"

No. Please don't let it be Mr. Gorgeous-eyes. I lowered my hands and my gaze. Those sure looked like his shoes. Expensive leather. Slowly, I raised my eyes. His trousers were perfectly tailored, as was his jacket. Broad chest. Classic, understated tie. As an archivist I knew that stories revealed themselves in the details.

Having grown up surrounded by the wealthy, I recognized his type. New money had more flash and sparkle. The attire of the insanely rich was less rigid—they played by their own rules and were often more than a little eccentric. This man was from old money, but I guessed he worked to maintain it. There was nothing soft about him. Not his jaw, not his expression while he waited for my response.

I met his gaze. "Not really, but I will be."

He stood there frowning down at me.

When he didn't say anything, I added, "It didn't go the way I'd hoped it would."

He nodded.

I continued, "I didn't handle it as well as I could have." Some of what I'd said was still echoing in my head. No matter how disappointed I was, I should have told Clay that I hadn't meant it when I'd said I wished it had been him and not Collin. I wasn't proud of how I'd imploded and run rather than stayed and countered his fantasy with reality.

"My guess is that it wasn't entirely your fault."

"Kind of you to say, but I expected better from myself." I swallowed hard. "My brother was no different than he's always been. Me? I thought I'd gotten to a point where I could speak rationally to him. I've been working on this project—" I stopped there. "You don't want to hear this."

He didn't protest that he did. If anything, his frown deepened. Was there a chance I was blocking his path? I glanced around. No, if his goal was the elevator there was plenty of room for him to pass.

The longer he stood there just looking down at me, the more confused I became. My body didn't care that he might be about to tell me he misplaced his wallet and was about to accuse me of taking it. No, I was sure the look in his eye was desire even though his lips were pressed together in a stern line. My heart was beating fast and my face flushed.

I wanted to shake him and demand he say something.

I wanted to wrap my arms around his neck, slide myself up against him, and kiss the anger right out of him.

"Would you like to grab a coffee?" he asked.

"With you?" I brought a hand up to smack my own forehead.

"Yes." A slight smile stretched his lips. "My name is Benjamin Drover." He held out his hand.

"Caterina." My hand shook when his closed around it. How was it possible for the touch of a stranger to feel so familiar? "Caterina Landon."

His grip tightened ever so slightly. "Single?"

"Painfully so," I joked then gasped as it came out much less humorously than I'd intended. I pulled my hand free from his. "Kidding. Perfectly happy figuring out things on my own." When he simply held my gaze again, I couldn't hold back, "And you?"

"Widower."

Widower? My heart went out to him. "I'm sorry."

He shrugged. "It's been over a year."

"Was she—is she the reason you're here?" It made sense that she would be. Clay's foundation was known for helping support families. He didn't appear in need of financial support, but loss hit a person on many levels.

"Yes." Those intense eyes of his held mine. "But I stayed to make sure you're okay."

He meant it.

I swayed on my feet. I'd dated men who'd been openly flirtatious. Some had said all the right things until they got what they wanted. None had stayed.

Not the men in my life.

Not a single member of my family.

I blinked back tears and waved my hand in Benjamin's direction. "Sorry, on any other day I would have said yes." My face warmed and I quickly corrected, "To coffee."

There it was, that faint smile. "Coffee was all I offered."

A smile tugged at my lips. "Either way, I'm going to pass. It's been a long day."

"You shouldn't be alone."

Wait, was he attracted to me or simply concerned for a stranger? My pride kicked in. "I don't need you to babysit me. I don't need anyone."

"So angry. You sound like me."

"I'm not—" I was ready with a snarky retort but then remembered he'd lost his wife. Did it really matter what he thought of me? What was the likelihood that we'd ever see each other again? Zero. "You're right. I'm angry. I have the right to be." I sighed. "But I don't want to be anymore."

Those dark eyes of his were impossible to look away from. Could he see my very soul? It felt as if he could. "We have that in common as well."

Was he referring to losing his wife? "Whoever said time heals all wounds was full of shit."

He chuckled at that and this time his smile reached his eyes. "I'm in full agreement." After a pause he said, "I wanted to punch your brother, but a lot of my anger has nothing to do with him."

He was saying what I needed to hear. I clenched my

hands at my sides. "I wish I could say the same. I could—about the punching part. If I were the type to punch anyone. I'm not. I'm more the type to write out all of my feelings in a letter I tear up without sending."

"Maybe you should send those letters."

"Maybe you shouldn't hold your punches."

"I don't lose control."

"Whoops, then I guess we aren't twins because I totally lost my shit a few minutes ago." I shook my head. Why were all of my jokes coming out like calls for help? Because he had broad shoulders? That wasn't the kind of strength I was yearning to find. "Well, thank you for making sure I'm okay. I am."

"Lunch." He voiced his offer more like a command.

"I'm not hungry."

"Shots of tequila until we fuck and pass out?"

I wrinkled my nose. "That's the best you have?"

The look in his eyes told me he was having fun with me. "A man has to ask."

"Does he, though?" I smiled.

His expression turned serious again. "Dinner."

I tilted my head to one side. "Why do I have the feeling you're not used to women saying no to you?"

"Why do I have the feeling you want to say yes?"

"I'm a hot mess in my head." I cringed as the admission poured out of me. "We're talking serious abandonment issues."

"I'm a miserable bastard." He raised and lowered a shoulder. "Lately I fucking hate everyone."

"We sound perfect for each other." My delivery was off once again. A group of people walked by and I took that as my cue to go. "It was nice to meet you, Benjamin Drover."

I might have been seeing what I wanted to, but he looked like he didn't want our exchange to end. "I'm sure our paths will cross again."

"I'm never coming back here."

"Did he hurt you?"

I blinked and looked away. "People can only hurt you if you give them the power to."

Embarrassed by how much I'd shared, I walked away.

He didn't follow, but I didn't expect him to.

Chapter Three

Benjamin

I'VE NEVER BEEN a violent man, but if Clay had been within reach I might have unleashed some of my anger with my fist on his face. If he ever touched her I'll kill him.

Prison will be worth it.

I glanced down at my watch and cursed. It was already late enough that I'd missed the first of the calls I'd planned. I headed back to my car and had just pulled out of the parking garage when a call came in from my father. Letting it go to voicemail was not an option since he would only call again. "Hi, Dad."

"Benjamin, how did it go with Clay Landon?"

"Not as smoothly as I'd planned. I'll be giving Tasha's lawyer a call tomorrow."

"What happened?"

"I really don't want to talk about it, Dad."

"Do you want me to handle the donation?"

I sighed audibly. My parents hadn't been helicopter parents until Tasha died. I blamed it on the fact that my parents had retired. Together they'd successfully run our family's luxury goods brand: Drover. They dealt in diamonds and fine jewelry. I could have followed in their footsteps but the world of fashion had never held my attention. Instead, I'd gambled my trust fund on quantum mechanics becoming a part of everyday technology. It was headed that way and the industry had proven highly lucrative. The most precise timekeepers in the world were atomic clocks and even they would soon become a dinosaur as our understanding of atoms deepened. Exciting stuff.

The industry was booming. Encryption? Quantum keys were uncrackable. Medical industry? Entangled enhanced microscopes, faster computing, and AI were poised to bring the kind of change that the industrial age brought to manufacturing. My company Drover Ware didn't have household brand recognition, but its innovations were needed for so many product lines that did.

You would think that would be what my parents wanted to talk about—but no. Suddenly, now that they had too much time on their hands, they were concerned about my happiness and bonding. The week after Tasha's death my parents had come to my apartment with food my mother claimed to have made.

I didn't call out the lie, but her cooking tasted remarkably like that of their long-time, live-in cook. Running the family company had left no time for things like cooking, cleaning, or raising me. I understood the necessity of fifteen-hour workdays, especially after I started my own company.

What I didn't understand was their current need to pretend we were closer than we actually were. They were my parents. I loved them. Did we need to speak daily? Not in my opinion. They'd raised me to be an independent problem solver so why did they suddenly believe I needed their help? Success-wise, I'd already surpassed what would have been possible had I stayed with the family business.

I certainly didn't require hand-holding when it came to dealing with a lawyer. "I'm all set, Dad."

"Your mother and I were thinking about coming to Boston on Wednesday. I've made reservations already. We'd like to see you."

"I wish you hadn't. This is a busy week for me."

"Too busy for us?"

A guilt trip? Really? Over a dinner? I could believe an alien race had snatched my parents and replaced them before I could believe this was actually who my parents had become. "It's midweek, Dad."

"We can change it to the weekend if you'd prefer."

"How about if I call you when things calm down? We'll pick a day then."

"We'll be in town on Wednesday. I'll send you the information."

"Wednesday isn't—" He ended the call before I had a chance to finish. Fuck.

I was still in a sour mood when I strode into my office, told my PA I didn't want to be interrupted, and slammed my door. Regardless of what was going on in the world, work brought me peace and focus. It was unusual for whatever was bothering me outside the office to follow me inside. I sat at my desk to make the phone calls I'd planned, but didn't.

The door to my office opened. Martina Hudson, my business partner and head of my research and development department, walked in looking as disheveled in jeans and a T-shirt as she always did. Little had changed about her since we'd met at Princeton. My guess was those were even the same sneakers she'd worn back then.

I'd known from the first class of hers I had taken that she wasn't enjoying her role as Princeton's youngest tenured professor. She was brilliant, but painfully awkward in social situations. College kids, especially those from wealthy parents, could be ruthless. I felt bad enough for her that I stayed after class one day and offered to show her how to effectively back down assholes—and a friendship was born.

When I started Drover Ware I knew its success would rely on the team I gathered around me. I lured Martina away from academia, a switch she said she had yet to regret. Money didn't matter to her, but funds supported her research and at Drover Ware she had access to nearly limitless funding. The return for her work consistently outweighed the investment.

She took a seat in one of the chairs in front of my desk. "So your mother called me. Looks like we're having dinner with them on Wednesday."

"You might be—I am not." I slapped a hand on my desktop. "In fact, why are you? You realize you can just say no."

She shrugged. "I like your parents. They took me shopping last week for a TV when I told them I didn't have one.

I don't have the heart to tell them I don't watch TV. It's kind of nice to have someone care. Your mother wants to find me a nice husband. I didn't tell her I'm into women."

"My parents have lost their minds. Don't encourage this phase they're going through. They'll find a hobby soon and forget about both of us."

"You say that like it would be a good thing. I, for one, don't want to be forgotten. Am I too old for your parents to adopt?"

I gave her a look that I hoped would shut the topic down.

She rolled her eyes skyward. "Hey, you don't want them and I don't have parents so really would sharing them be so hard?"

I sighed. "You know what? Go to dinner with them. Have my mother start hunting for the perfect wife for you. Start your own family and you can all spend the holidays together."

"You're in a mood today, but we all expected you to be."

I stood and growled. "And why is that?"

"Because going to the Landon Foundation meant you had to think about Tasha and you've tried to spend the last year not doing that."

"My mood has nothing to do with Tasha."

"Okay."

"I've put that part of my life behind me."

"Slammed that door shut. Got it."

"I can be in a bad mood without it having anything to do with her. Marrying her was a mistake, just not one she gave me time to rectify."

"Ouch. It's settled then, you've completely moved on."

"I have."

"So making Drover Ware your new home has nothing to do with her death?"

"I've been very clear about that."

"You have. It's just sad to watch you become someone who has no life outside of this building."

"Like you're any different?"

"I go out."

"Dinner with my parents doesn't count."

"Now you're just being a dick. Sit your ass down and tell me what's really going on."

I wouldn't have tolerated talk like that from anyone else, not even my parents, but I was the one who had taught Martina to be more assertive. I was kind of proud of her when she stood up for herself even when it happened at the most annoying times. I sat, not because she'd told me to, but because I realized I wasn't as in control as I prided myself for being. "I met someone today—"

"You met someone? No wonder you don't want to talk about Tasha."

"Not like that." I ran a hand through my hair. "Forget I said anything."

"No, hang on. This is the first woman you've mentioned since . . ."

"Stop."

She did for a zeptosecond. "What's her name?"

Even as I shook my head, I said, "Caterina Landon."

"Landon—as in the Landon Foundation."

"She's Clay's sister. Estranged. I don't know the details. He wants nothing to do with her. I met her on the way in. She was nervous. When I spoke to her afterward she seemed . . . devastated. I don't know what he said to her, but he's lucky I don't."

Martina crossed one leg over the other and leaned forward. "I like her already."

"Based on what?"

"You asked her out."

"I did."

"And she said no."

"She did."

Martina smiled. "It took long enough for you to find one."

"Find one?"

"Someone who could make you feel something again."

"What I felt was pity for her. It was obvious she cared about someone who didn't care at all about her."

"And you remember that feeling."

My hands fisted. "You're a brilliant mathematician, Martina, but you don't know shit about me if you think Tasha hurt me."

Martina nodded and sat back. "I can't wait to tell your parents about Caterina."

"You wouldn't—" I stopped when her smile widened. "And yet I'm the dick?"

"Did you get her number?"

"No."

"I'm sure it wouldn't be that hard to locate Clay Landon's sister."

"If I wanted to, which I don't."

"If you did want to, you could send her a gift with a note saying you hope she's having a better day."

"I have no interest in doing anything like that."

"Flowers are overdone. Send her something unique. Not suggestive. Not temporary. Something she could pull out at your fiftieth anniversary and say it swayed her into giving you a chance."

"Martina?"

"Yes?"

"Don't go to dinner with my parents. They're beginning to affect you."

"In a good way. They've realized that no amount of money is as important as the connections we foster with the ones we love. It's why they want to spend time with you now. They want to know you."

"It's a little late for that."

"Is it? I was snapped up from child services as soon as my IQ was discovered. People always cared more about what I could do than how I felt. I was totally alone before I met you, and I thought I always would be. You were the first one who saw me. I'm grateful for that and that you've become the family I never had. I love you."

I met her gaze and grudgingly conceded, "I'll go with you to dinner with my parents."

She clapped her hands together. "Thank you. I live for when your mother tries to teach me recipes she just learned from the internet and doesn't fully understand. She wants to mother someone so badly. I'd probably let her diaper me if she asked."

I groaned. "Oh, my God, stop. How do I get that image out of my head?"

"By thinking about Caterina and what you'll send her?"

I made a dismissive sound, but even as I did, an image of Caterina standing outside the elevator with her hands over her face haunted me. She'd put her heart on the line only to have it handed back to her in shards. I did know that feeling. *People can only hurt you if you give them the power to.* I understood that as well.

Caring about anyone enough that they could topple me? Been there, done that. Not eager to repeat the experience. Still, I never could walk past someone I knew was in need. "What gift says 'You'll get through this' without implying that she should contact me?"

Martina smiled and stood. "I love that you believe you don't want to see her again. Or maybe you just want me to believe that. Either way, the actual gift won't matter as much as the note you send with it."

"I'm not looking for a relationship."

"Me neither, but you're talking to someone who knew you BT. It's time."

Before Tasha. "I'm happy with my life the way it is, and seriously this woman doesn't matter to me beyond that I was concerned for her."

"Try to remember that when she calls to thank you and you find yourself asking her out again."

I stood and crossed over to where Martina was standing. My parents hadn't given me a sister, but Princeton had. I held out my arms for a hug. She stepped in for one and I said, "I love you too, Martin."

She pinched my side as she stepped out of the hug. "That's the thanks I get, Bend-over?"

I barked out a laugh. "Don't you have work waiting for you somewhere?"

"I do," she said and walked to the door. "Can I tell your PA the storm has passed and it's safe to enter your office again?"

I did feel lighter. "You may, but also tell her to give me a few minutes first."

She brought a hand to her heart. "So you can order the gift you don't want anyone to know you're sending?"

I pointed toward the door. "Get out before I change my mind about that dinner."

She skirted out with a laugh.

Alone, I sent a text to my father. **See you on Wednesday.**

His answer was immediate. **Good. Your mother asked Martina to join us.**

I know. She told me. Is Mom really trying to find a husband for her?

Would it be a problem if she is?

Not if Mom broadens the dating pool for her. Martina prefers women.

Oh. I'll tell your mother. Does she have a type?

I knew my father would take the revelation in stride. I would have encouraged Martina to tell my parents herself, but when it came to my parents she worried about doing anything to offend them. My parents had their faults, but being accepting of differences had never been one of them. They genuinely cared for Martina.

Someone who likes dogs. She's always wanted one.

Our neighbor has a dog walker who is cute. I'll see if she's single.

Dad. Don't walk around the neighborhood asking women if they're single.

Right. I'll let your mother handle it.

Smart. I have some calls to make. See you Wednesday.

Love you.

My fingers hovered over my phone. On one hand, being reminded by Martina that not everyone had parents made me feel that I should try harder with mine. On the other hand, they'd chosen a tough year to go all mushy on me. I couldn't not respond with something so I wrote: **Love you too.**

I slid my phone back into my jacket pocket and stuck my head out the door. I had people waiting to hear from me, but there was something I needed to do first.

"Harami, I'd like to send something to Caterina Landon but I don't have an address or phone number. Will you locate both for me?"

"Absolutely. Does she work for the Landon Foundation?"

"Not that I'm aware of, but she's Clay Landon's sister."

"Oh, I didn't know he had one."

Not surprising. "Just get me that information."

"Absolutely. I'll message you with it shortly."

I nodded and closed the door again. Harami had been

my PA since day one of Drover Ware. She juggled caring for two children and a husband battling cancer, yet somehow she remained reliable and made sure if she took a day off her work didn't suffer.

A year ago, when I'd stumbled, she'd made sure no one knew. Her high salary reflected my gratitude. You could teach a person how to run an office, but you couldn't teach them how to be loyal. Trustworthy people were a rare find both in business and in life.

Returning to my desk I did an internet search for gifts that make women smile. I scrolled past the very personal gadgets that required batteries, until I found a site that filled small boxes with individual chocolates. Each box had a different label on it. I read the first few: Open this when you're sad. Open this one when you're happy. Open this one when it's raining. Open this one when it's sunny.

Cute.

Designed to cheer a person up.

Everyone likes chocolate.

Perfect.

I contacted the seller and asked for the cost of same day delivery. They said it wasn't possible. I quoted an amount I knew would change the seller's mind and they agreed to it. I told them I'd send an address shortly.

Before I had a chance to make my first business call, Harami sent me Caterina's number and home address, as well as her latest job assignment archiving family records for a small town outside of Boston. Interesting.

A quick google of the address revealed she lived an hour

or so outside of the city. Her home was a modest one in a neighborhood with small yards and inexpensive cars. It was my understanding that Clay had inherited his fortune. Why hadn't his sister? Although it was difficult to do, my opinion of Clay fell even lower. What kind of man doesn't take care of his family?

The same kind that pretends they don't exist.

I forwarded Caterina's information to the woman who made the little boxes and felt good about my decision to send the gift. There wasn't anything I could do about her family situation, but if nothing else, Caterina would have a reason to smile that day.

I turned my attention back to business and only stopped about once an hour to wonder what she'd do when she received the gift.

Chapter Four

Caterina

THAT EVENING I parked my car in my driveway and sat there for a moment. After leaving Clay's office I had returned to work, hoping it would help clear my head. I should have said no to the historical group that had called me. On a consultant basis, I'd worked for major museums. I'd also helped organize and digitize old records at more than one hospital. The money I'd been offered for my current assignment hadn't even been that good.

So why had I agreed to it?

The woman who'd contacted me had said, "Our exhibit will be about more than resurrecting the history of the region. We want to reunite people with their ancestors and show them how we are all much more connected than we realize. This is about family—the ones we love today, the ones we've lost, and those we never knew we had."

Family. There was an overwhelming lure to believing in the resiliency of it. I'd been told my responsibility was to simply digitize the information into a searchable database. However, as soon as I dug in I realized more was possible.

They couldn't afford the type of hours involved, so I'd volunteered my free time as well to organize fragments of family trees until they began to fit together like a beautifully complex puzzle. I read journals, birth records, death notices, news articles until each name I recorded into the database had a story and a connection to the community. The story they told was of immigration, struggle, determination, loss, and survival.

If they could go through what they did and not only survive—but thrive, so could I. Reading over all the resolved feuds had given me some unrealistic hope that something like that was possible in my own life. When I thought about how unable I'd been to hear anything Clay had to say I slumped in my seat.

In my head I was stronger and braver than what I'd brought to his office.

I let myself out of my car and looked up at the sky. And, seriously, tossing Mr. Gorgeous-eyes into the mix was just cruel on your part. I did not need a witness to my meltdown.

I smiled as a thought occurred to me. I did appreciate him acting like he was interested in me, though. So, thanks for that. I guess sending me gorgeous men isn't the worst way you could show you care.

I had no idea if God ever heard me, but I started talking to him/her in my head during the darkest years of my life and those conversations still comforted me. When I felt most alone I needed to know I wasn't. And I was alone most of the time.

It wasn't that people didn't like me. I could strike up a

conversation with complete strangers with ease. What I couldn't do was maintain more than a superficial friendship. Those required trust and I didn't have a lot of that left.

As I approached my house, I squared my shoulders and told myself to think of something happy. It was then that I spotted a large delivery box. I hadn't ordered anything recently so I double-checked the address on it. It was for me. The return address was a place a few states away. Linda's Creations. Never heard of it.

I picked up the box. It was light. I shook it but doing so didn't reveal its contents. Deciding it was a promotional offer of something, I unlocked the door and carried the box into the living room.

Tired, I put the box down on my coffee table and started to walk away from it. Whatever was in it didn't matter. I only made it halfway to the kitchen before I turned and looked back at the box.

What if it was something wonderful? Something I didn't know I wanted?

Really, what was the likelihood of that?

Still, I walked back to the box and sat on the couch beside it. The alternative to opening it was rummaging through my refrigerator alone, throwing together whatever was in there, only to come back out and have dinner alone while reading a book about people who were living much more exciting lives than I was.

I stood and pulled a thick piece of tape free, then yanked it off the top of the box. It opened to reveal lavender tissue paper that I threw aside, uncovering about fifty tiny square boxes. I picked one up and read the label on it aloud, "Open when you miss me." I opened it. Inside was one Hershey's Kiss chocolate.

I put the box aside and began to read the labels on the other boxes. "Open when you decide you want to meet my mother. Open when you realize you love me. Open when you wish I was there with you."

Okay, this was definitely meant for someone else.

I hunted through the packaging for a note. It had my name on it. When I opened it and saw who it was from my mouth dropped open. Benjamin Drover?

Mr. Gorgeous-eyes?

The note was typed rather than handwritten. It read: I hope this makes you smile. After his signature he had written his cell phone number.

I read the note a second time then went back to reading the messages on the labels. "Open this one when you decide to have my children. Open this one when you want a key to my place."

Wow. That's a lot.

I put the note back in the box, closed it, and walked to the other side of the room. It wasn't funny if his intention had been to make a joke out of our attraction. If it wasn't a joke, it was too much to be romantic.

I double-checked the lock on my door.

He didn't look like the type of man who would stalk a woman. Actually I had no idea what that kind of man would look like. Maybe they looked exactly like him.

Maybe he really wasn't used to women saying no to him.

I put the box near the door and told myself I would toss it out in the trash in the morning. The next morning, I left the box near the door, but swore I'd dispose of it that evening. That evening, I moved the box back to my coffee table and read all the labels. Some were sweet. "Open this one when you're sad." I opened it and ate the chocolate inside. "Open this one when you're happy." I put that one aside and reached for another. "Open this one when you can't stop thinking about me." I opened that one as well and scarfed the chocolate inside.

"Open this one when it's sunny." I looked out the window. The sun was beginning to go down, but I decided it still counted and opened that box too.

"Open this one when you're embarrassed by how much you want to jump me." I pushed that box into an ever-growing pile of ones that went too far. "You need an ego check, sir. I said no."

When I read the next label, my hand started shaking so much I dropped the box. "Open this one when you realize you're my forever."

Tears entered my eyes and I shoved the rest of the boxes away. I wanted to be someone's forever. I wanted it more than I'd ever allowed myself to admit.

Was it possible to hate someone I hardly knew? If so, I hated Benjamin Drover for making me face something I'd been denying.

I don't want to be alone anymore.

I'm not happy with the way things are. I want a family, friends, people who care about me.

I hate that my brother pretends I don't exist.

I hate that I don't even know where my other brother is.

I don't want to be this version of me anymore, but I don't even know where to begin to be anything else.

With that, I stuffed the small boxes back into the package they'd come in and tossed it into one of my closets. I closed the door on it like I'd closed the door on so much from my childhood. Wishing things were different had never made them better.

And I didn't believe it ever would.

I can't go on this way. I thought about the things I wanted and which parts I could change. The ladies from the historical group I was working for had invited me out several times but I had yet to meet them anywhere. Sure they were all over the age of fifty, but they were always laughing and upbeat. I could use some of that in my life. I paced from one room to another. Staying home, avoiding social situations, and refusing to let anyone too close was how I'd gotten where I was.

I'm not doing that anymore.

I found my phone and called Lorraine, the woman who had initially hired me. When we'd first met she'd introduced herself as a retired homemaker. She'd stayed home to raise three children, all of whom had gone to college and had successful careers. Parenting, she said, is never done. Although there had been a span of her life when all of her children were adults and her home had felt empty, once they'd started marrying and having children of their own she'd happily become a part-time granny nanny. There was always something going on at her house and I enjoyed listening to the stories she shared about her family.

"Lorraine," I said in a thick voice, then cleared my throat and started over. "It's Caterina."

As always there was a smile in her voice. "I was just going to call you. Tell me this is about going to Boston with us tomorrow."

Just do it. "It's about going to Boston with you tomorrow." I swallowed hard. "I want to."

"Really?" she said with such pleasure I had to blink back tears. "Your ears must have been ringing. Emmie and I were just talking about how much we'd like you there. You work so hard and this is becoming a dream trip to the city. Emmie's nephew drives a limo. When he heard we were going to take the train in from the Park-n-Ride he offered to drive us around for the day. We're going to window shop on Newbury Street, stop by a mall, then we have reservations at an Italian restaurant in Beacon Hill. It's impossible to get a reservation there, but Keiona's brother-in-law was a dishwasher there for a long time. The hostess still has a crush on him so he was able to set it up for us. He booked a table for four just in case you changed your mind."

My heart was racing. I don't know if I'd ever been as nervous accepting to go out with a man. Until just then Lorraine, Emmie, and Keiona had been people I categorized as temporary associations. When I completed the job with them, I had accepted that they would fade out of my life. It was a pattern I'd become comfortable with. Each new assignment brought people into my life that I had no reason to see again once I moved on to the next job.

Did it have to be that way? These ladies lived one town

over from here. They were all so nice. I needed nice in my life. "That all sounds fantastic. Thank you so much for inviting me."

"Since we have the limo we don't have to worry as much about walking so wear something nice. The restaurant is upscale. Real napkins, more forks than you need—that kind of thing. It'll be fun to pretend we're rich for a day."

I almost blurted that there was nothing fun about being wealthy, but I held back. Even though I'd walked away from my family's money, it was risky to tell people that I had rich relatives. Lorraine might not care, but she might tell someone who might tell someone who might see it as an opportunity. Would Clay even pay a ransom for my safety? I had no idea, but I never wanted to put him to that test. "I can't wait," I said, because I didn't know what else to say.

"We're meeting at Keiona's house at eleven. Would you like me to swing by and pick you up?"

"That's not necessary." Trust was hard for me. There were more nights than I wanted to admit when I still woke up from nightmares that were terrifying because they were based on memories rather than my imagination. I didn't like to be anywhere I couldn't leave easily so I always drove myself and had a plan for how to get away if I needed to. I groaned. If I couldn't trust someone like Lorraine, who would I ever trust? I couldn't change the past, but I had to believe I could make changes in me. "Actually, I would like that very much."

"Great. Be ready for ten forty-five. I'll text you when I'm on my way."

Chapter Five

Benjamin

MARTINA WAS ALREADY seated with my parents at a table in an Italian restaurant that overlooked the Boston Common in Beacon Hill. My father stood as I approached and shook my hand then hesitated. I sat before he could do something awkward like hug me. "Mom. Martina. Sorry I'm late."

"If you didn't want to be late, you wouldn't be," my mother said. Hers was the voice I often heard in my head when I was annoyed.

Martina smiled and touched my arm. "I'm surprised you didn't cancel. The way you've been moping the last few days I was sure you would."

I arched an eyebrow at her. "I don't mope."

My mother's expression softened. "I know this is a hard time for you."

I opened my napkin and laid it across my lap. "It's not and I'm fine."

"Let the boy have a moment, Margaret." He waved to someone across the dining area. A young woman in a chef's double-breasted white jacket nodded and walked to our table. "Suzanne Bailey's Lobster gnocchi is to die for. Her father runs our favorite restaurant in the North End. Suzanne this is my son, Benjamin, and his business partner, Martina. They are not a couple. They're both very single."

"Dad, stop."

My mother shook her head, but she was smiling. "Suzanne, please excuse my husband. Martina is like a daughter to us and the clock is ticking for us as far as having grandchildren while we're young enough to enjoy them."

Martina gave me a mortified look that reflected how I felt. I probably should have warned her that I'd updated my parents on her preference. I'd imagined the reveal being a lot more subtle. "Oh."

Suzanne smiled graciously. "Although I'm flattered, I'm currently dating someone." She had the grace to wink at my father. "I'll keep them both in mind, though, if it doesn't work out."

Looking pleased with himself, my father sat back and asked the chef if she used her father's style as an inspiration for her own menu. The question brought a glow to the woman's face. "There is a little bit of both of my parents in every dish I make. My father is Irish, but he met my mother and her family when he was just beginning his chef career. He took their recipes and made them his own—just as I've done. For us, food is how we celebrate who we are as well as show the ones we love that we celebrate them as well." She turned to my mother and asked, "Do you have a favorite family recipe?"

I coughed.

Martina kicked my leg under the table. "She does. Margaret, tell her about your Chicken Cacciatore. It's delicious."

That perked up Suzanne's interest. She asked my mother, "Do you use pancetta?"

When my mother hesitated, I said, "She uses prosciutto instead but it works." I couldn't let Martina be my parents' only good child.

Suzanne didn't look nearly as impressed by my contribution as she had Martina's. She directed her next question to her. "Do you like to cook as well?"

Martina blushed. "I'm more comfortable cooking up lemmas than recipes."

The chef tipped her head in question.

Looking awkward and embarrassed, Martina clarified, "A lemma is a statement that has been proven true and can aid in proving another statement true." She grimaced as if her next statement was something that required an apology. "I'm a mathematician."

Suzanne's eyebrows rose. "Smart is sexy."

Martina sat up a little straighter and released my arm. "I always thought so. I mean . . . hoped so."

A movement across the room caught Suzanne's attention. She apologized and motioned to her staff that she was on her way. With one last smile at Martina, she rushed away.

"So you told them," Martina muttered to me.

Beneath my breath I answered, "I thought it would help."

An expensive bottle of wine was delivered to our table.

My mother looked it over then said, "She seems lovely. We'll have to come back. Perhaps in a few weeks. Martina, you and I could go shopping first. Get you into a nice dress, have our hair done." She glanced down at Martina's hands. "Our nails as well."

I laughed at the shocked expression on Martina's face. She was the one who'd said she wanted to be mothered.

My father gave me the warning look that if ignored was always followed by a lecture on behavior. I could have told him I was too old to lecture, but I doubted he'd ever see me in that light.

My mother was smoothing things over with Martina by the time I looked back at them. To understand my mother, a person would have to know she'd been groomed from birth to find a wealthy husband. When she'd first married my father, she'd been the perfect little wife until he'd told her he needed more. He wanted a partner in business, pleasure, and parenting. As my mother tells it he told her to step up or step off. His version painted him in a more supportive light. The truth was somewhere in the middle. Either way, she'd been raised to think men cared more about the details than the substance, and that side of her surfaced from time to time.

My father wasn't what most would consider a romantic man. He didn't make grand gestures or make his feelings for my mother public. However, he loved her on her best and worst days. They could always be found together, working on something one or both of them was interested in, and every once in a while, if one watched for it they would reach out and link hands. Their loyalty to each other trumped whatever differences or disagreements they had.

I blamed them for how easily I'd believed Tasha when she'd said she loved me. The word meant something in my family. It hadn't to her.

I should have been relieved that Caterina hadn't bothered to call to thank me for the gift I'd sent her. The whole situation was a clusterfuck. Tasha's lawyer had informed me that her final wishes didn't allow for me to choose a different charity. After contacting Clay Landon my lawyer informed me that Clay would still only accept the donation if I attended one of his fucking surviving spouse support meetings—and that wasn't going to happen.

If I didn't know how easily he could afford any legal fight I could bring, I would have gone that route. Until I figured out another way around, I was stuck in donation limbo.

Getting involved with the sister of a man whose very name already annoyed me would have been a headache. Still, would it have killed her to thank me for the gift?

A note.

A text.

Anything that assured me it hadn't been sent to one of her neighbors accidently.

My attention was brought back to the present when my mother nudged my father. "Say something to him."

My father cleared his throat. "How you're feeling is normal. It'll get easier."

Martina smacked my arm. "Will you just tell them?"

"There's nothing to tell."

Looking me straight in the eye, she said, "You're not upset about Tasha. You met someone. Tell them."

"Benjamin, that's welcome news," my father said.

"What's her name?" My mother was beaming like I'd just announced an engagement.

Martina was unfazed by the glare I shot her as I said, "Her name doesn't matter because she doesn't."

"Her name is Caterina Landon," Martina supplied.

"As in the Landon Foundation?" my father asked.

I splayed my hands in the air and addressed Martina. "What are you doing?"

"Helping you realize you should apologize."

Oh. That drained away my irritation. I did owe her one, but not in front of my parents. My parents didn't do apologies or drama. We also didn't discuss my social life. Ever. I'd never doubted that my parents loved me, but we'd all been careful to stay in our own lane. "I'm sure no one wants to hear about some random woman I'll never see again."

Martina sighed and turned to my mother. "He asked her out but she turned him down."

"Oh, no." My mother brought a hand to her heart then turned to me. "I'm relieved to hear that you are getting back out there. You've been closed off for too long. Don't worry about this one. You'll meet someone else."

My father gave me a long look. "Unless you don't want to meet anyone else because there's something about this particular woman. What was she like?"

I groaned and sat back in my chair. "Could we not do this?"

Martina clapped her hands together. "I have an idea. Let's role play. Bennie look at me. Pretend I'm your mother. I want to know everything you're thinking and feeling. Spill."

There was something truly comical about how uncomfortable both of my parents looked. Even better, I was sure my expression mirrored the same. I chose honesty as my response. "If I said I'm sorry could we stop?"

My mother leaned toward me. "Benjamin, you have nothing to be sorry about."

I pinched the bridge of my nose then met Martina's gaze again. "I do. I shared something I shouldn't have. I am sorry. I did it with the best of intentions, but I was wrong."

Martina's shoulders relaxed and she nodded. "You're forgiven."

There was a brief pause to our conversation then my father said, "I have a feeling you will see this Caterina Landon again."

I shook my head and turned away. It was then that I saw Caterina being seated with three older women at a table on the other side of the restaurant. Her hair was tied back in a loose knot that left her neck deliciously exposed. Her dress was sleeveless with a modest neckline. Neither should have been enough to take my breath away as they did. When she laughed in response to something one of women said, I couldn't have looked away if someone had offered me billions to. "I have a feeling you're right."

"Oh my God, is that her?" Martina asked loud enough that I whipped around to wave a hand at her to stop.

My mother glanced at the group then back at me. "The one in the blue dress I hope."

A little devil in me wanted to claim Caterina was any of the other women from the group, but my first priority was figuring out my next step. I could deny it was her and simply not look in that direction again.

I glanced over at Caterina and conceded to myself that ignoring her was not a feasible option. Nor was lying. I turned back to the three people who were already far too involved in this. "It is her, but as Martina said—she said no. End of story."

"Did you send her a gift like we discussed?"

It was my turn to be irritated. "I apologized and you accepted. Call off the dogs."

Martina wrinkled her nose at me. "This isn't about torturing you." She looked at my parents then me again. "They want to know as well."

"They don't."

My father cut in. "Actually, we do. Your mother and I went to a communication coach and—"

"You went to what?" No. I wasn't swallowing that one.

"A communication coach. Your mother and I had gotten to a point where we had stopped having sex and neither of us could understand why."

"You really don't have to explain." Please, God, don't.

My father continued anyway. "Turned out we just needed to talk it out. The coach's methods worked so well, we told her about how we were sad that we rarely see you now. She said that happens when families don't talk openly as well. When you lost Tasha, we didn't know how to help you. We didn't know what to say or even if you wanted us to say anything so we said nothing. We're here to tell you that we love you. And that we want to be more a part of your life." His voice was thick with emotion and I wasn't prepared for how deeply that shook me.

This wasn't my family.

Or, at least, it never had been.

My mother reached over and laid her hand on mine. "Don't shut us out. If your father and I can learn how to share how we feel—you can as well. I know I wasn't a traditional mother. I didn't stick little notes in your lunch box or help you with homework. But I am so proud of the man you've become and I couldn't love you more than I do."

I let out a breath I hadn't realized I'd been holding.

Martina joked, "If you don't say something nice right now I'm claiming them as my own parents and tossing your butt to the curb because I'm about to start crying—that was so beautiful." She slapped my shoulder. "Just say you love them too."

"They know I do," I said a little defensively. Taking another deep, calming breath, I studied my parents' faces. They did know, didn't they? I cleared my throat. "I've never felt that you weren't amazing parents. I know exactly how lucky I am to have been raised by both of you. Maybe I don't say it easily, but you have to know I love you."

My mother's hand tightened on mine. "We do. Now tell us about that pretty young lady who can't keep her eyes off you. She certainly doesn't look like someone who isn't interested."

Don't look. Don't do it. I glanced over my shoulder because I couldn't not. When our eyes met our attraction hit me like a sucker punch. I tried to tell myself she wasn't any different than any other woman I'd ever found attractive, but that wasn't how it felt. It might have been my imagination, but she sure did look just as affected as I felt.

I forced myself to turn away from her again. "I asked her out, she said no. I sent her a gift, she didn't respond. I refuse to waste any more time."

"What did you send her?" my father asked.

Are we really doing this? We really were. With a sigh of resignation I took out my phone and opened the app to the store where I'd purchased the gift. It was easier to show them. "This. She seemed sad when we met and I was hoping it would cheer her up."

Martina took my phone right out of my hand and scrolled around the page. Her hand flew to her mouth and she handed my phone off to my mother who showed my father. I rolled my eyes skyward. Why were they all smiling? "What is so funny about sending boxes of chocolates?"

With a suddenly sympathetic expression, my mother asked, "Did you read what was printed on the boxes?"

"Of course. Something about opening them when she's sad and opening another when she's happy."

Shaking her head, Martina laughed and laid her hand on my arm again. "You should always scroll down to see what people say in the reviews. Also, you chose the 'getting serious' romance package. Holy shit, I'm trying to imagine what I would think if someone sent me this after meeting me once." She took the phone back and read aloud, "Open this one when you're ready to name our children. That's a little much, don't you think?"

My father coughed into his hand.

My mother looked like she was doing her best to not give in to a laugh as well.

I grabbed my phone back, read the labels on the boxes people had posted in their review photos and groaned. Sure as shit, there were different gift options and I'd chosen the 'getting serious' romance one. Oh, great, I won't have to wonder when to propose because I already sent her a box asking her to open it when she's ready for me to.

Fuck me.

"No need to see our communication coach. Looks like you're already putting your feelings right out there." There was a gurgle of laughter in my father's voice.

Despite being pissed with myself for making such a stupid move, it was nice to see my father relaxing enough to let his sense of humor out. Who knew he even had one?

My perfectly behaved mother pretended she was holding a fishing pole and was winding up the line. "Reel it in a little, Benjamin. Don't scare her off before we get our grandchildren—especially since. . ." She started laughing so hard she couldn't say it. "Especially since. . ."

"Mm-hmm. Since?"

She waved a hand, and collected herself enough to say, "Especially since you've already asked her to name them."

I covered my eyes with one hand and shook my head

while the three of them gave in to a fit of laughter. As they chortled, a laugh rumbled in my own chest. It really was the most ridiculous thing I'd ever done. Between laughs, I said, "At least I know why she didn't call me."

Martina leaned her head on my shoulder. "Bennie, I adore you, but I'm not taking dating tips from you."

My mother's hand flew to her throat. "Oh, looks like she just dropped her drink on herself. The poor thing."

I spun around again and sure enough she was standing and flapping the front of her dress as if to shake liquid free from it. A waiter rushed over with cloth napkins.

When Caterina's eyes met mine, her face flushed and she seemed to panic. She grabbed her purse, said something to the women at the table, and bolted for the door.

I rose to my feet.

"Go after her," my father urged.

"I-I—" was all I said before I did just that.

Chapter Six

Caterina

I PAUSED OUTSIDE the restaurant long enough to scan the area for Emmie's nephew, who was standing with the limo a short distance down the street. What I wanted to do was run to the limo and ask him to take me home—but I couldn't do that because he was also the ride for the other ladies.

I could use an app to call for a car for myself. I shouldn't have said, "I'll be right back," when I left the table. I'd made it seem like the wet spot on the front of my dress was the reason I'd bolted. I could tell them I was more drenched than I'd thought and I'd decided to go home, but they wouldn't let me leave like that. They'd be worried enough to come out and try to remedy the situation.

I couldn't tell them the truth. They'd been enjoying the restaurant, wondering aloud what it would be like to have the kind of money to eat there on a regular basis, and simply enjoying the end to what had been such a fun day.

I don't want to ruin that.

I'd felt trapped between disappointing them and facing a

situation I didn't want to. I never did well in those situations. My need to never again be anywhere I couldn't escape from overrode my determination to not give in to the panic again. It's what had driven me from Clay's office. It's what had me literally shaking and unsure of what to do next even though my rational brain knew I wasn't in any danger.

Benjamin might have sent me an overzealous gift, but he wasn't going to snatch me from the street. There was no white van poised to whisk me away in the middle of the night. I was safe and he was just a man I couldn't get out of my head.

Not that he was struggling with moving on. Single? My ass. I tried to tell myself it shouldn't matter to me. To be jealous would have required me letting someone close enough for me to care who they were with when they weren't with me and I didn't do that. So why had watching a woman hang all over Benjamin gut me? The couple with them shared enough features with him that my guess was they were his parents. I hated that it bothered me to see how much they liked the woman he was with.

I wished I'd never gone to see Clay. I'd liked myself a lot more before I'd reopened that old wound and met a man who had me so confused I thought I might get sick right there on the street.

I don't want to focus on what I don't have.

I've been down that road and it doesn't lead to anywhere good.

I'm out with friends, having a great day.

I need to allow myself to have this.

Breathe.

I can do this. I need to go back inside and pretend he's not there.

"Caterina."

Not even attempting a smile, I slowly turned to face him. "Benjamin. What a surprise."

He came to a stop close enough that I swayed a little toward him before gaining control of myself. "When I saw you leave—"

Here we go again. "You wanted to make sure I was okay." I referenced the wet skirt of my dress. "Outside of being a little drenched, I'm fine."

He pocketed his hands and rocked back on his heels. "About the gift I sent you."

"It was—a lot, but thank you." I took a step back.

His smile was charming and nonthreatening. "I should have read the description more carefully. I thought I'd ordered something a little less . . ."

"Creepy?"

"Yes. My goal was to make you smile, not double-check that your doors were locked."

That almost brought a smile to my face because the second part was exactly what it had done. He might have moved onto another woman but at least he wasn't as stalkerish as his gift had implied. It was a good thing, so why did it also make me sad? "Well, thank you for checking on me and for the chocolates. You can return to your date now."

"My date?" He glanced back at the restaurant. "Oh, Martina. She's my business partner."

Sure. "Whoever she is, I'm sure she's anxious for you to return. You seemed to be having a lot of fun together."

His mouth stretched in a grin. "And that bothered you?"

Hugging an arm around myself, I shook my head. "Not at all. I don't know you or her. Who you decide to let paw you in public is none of my business."

"I'll have to tell her that's how she comes across. Sending out mixed signals might be why she finds it hard to meet people. We are definitely not together."

"As I said, I don't care."

"That's disappointing."

"Excuse me?"

"Because I don't know you either, but I already don't want to see you with someone else."

My whole body warmed beneath his gaze. I was used to men who flattered, but this was different. This was an acknowledgement of something more primal. Raw. Possessive. Exciting in a dangerous way. "That's—that's—"

"More honest than I probably should be, but whatever this is between us, it's different enough that we should explore it."

My throat tightened. "I'm not interested in exploration. I'm hoping to find something a little more meaningful than that."

His grin faded. "Because of your abandonment issues?"

I sucked in a harsh breath. "If you're hoping I'll agree to a date with you, you played this all wrong. Throwing something I'm embarrassed about back in my face isn't how to win me over."

Our connection was so strong I couldn't look away even as I tried to sound uninterested. He took a moment before saying, "I don't want a date. A date lately is just meaningless conversation, a nice meal, good sex, and please don't stay overnight. I want to know what has you looking like you're on the run. I want to know you."

His claim echoed through me. Letting people close enough to know you meant letting them close enough to hurt you. My heart was racing in my chest, partly from the sexual tension in the air and partly from an all-too-common panic I suffered from. "Because you think I need help?"

"Because I can't stop thinking about you." He stayed where he was, hands in his pockets, confident and relaxed. "If you're really not interested, say it and you won't hear from me again." His eyes held a fire that matched the one he'd lit in me.

I didn't say I didn't want to see him again. It wasn't true. I wasn't brave enough to voice the opposite, though, so I just stood there staring up at him.

"Let's get you out of that dress."

My jaw dropped open. "I don't know what you think—"

"There's a clothing shop right around the corner." His smile returned. "I thought you might be more comfortable in something dry."

"Oh," I said in a breathless tone. "I would be."

He offered me his arm. "Then let's go shopping."

Unsure of what taking his arm would imply, I hesitated. "I can buy my own clothing."

His expression turned serious again. "What are you

afraid of?"

I could have lied. Had he been almost anyone else I might have. He had this way, though, of looking right past my defenses into my soul. As much as it was scary to feel exposed, I also didn't want to shut him out. Blinking away the tears I hated for surfacing just then, I said, "I've been in situations where I wasn't in control and—"

"And someone hurt you."

"Yes. Maybe not in the way you're thinking, but yes." God, I didn't want to open that door, but he claimed to want to know the real me. There I was in all my ugly, neurotic, panicky glory. "No, I don't want to talk about it, but it does still affect me. When I feel trapped, I panic." I attempted a smile. "I'm working on it."

His nostrils flared but his voice was gentle when he said, "Was your brother involved?"

I closed my eyes briefly, as I sought to remain calm. "He denies it, but I know he was. It was a long time ago, though, and I'm really trying to put it behind me."

He nodded and neither of us spoke for a moment. A small smile pulled at his lips. "So, I should stop trying to get you out of that dress?"

The flirty humor was a much-needed relief. Two could play at this game. "I am pretty wet." I didn't realize how that might sound until it came out of my mouth and my cheeks warmed.

Desire flared in his eyes again, but this time I didn't feel I had to run from it. I'd set a boundary and he'd respected it. In response, my panic was receding. "If you're hoping I'll agree to go anywhere you ask, you played this all right," he said.

The look we exchanged was intense. It cut through the pain and the pleasure to what was impossible to deny—whatever this was it definitely was different. "I might be up for a little exploration." I pinched an inch of air. "Like this much. Just a walk to the clothing shop and back."

He held out his arm to me again. "I'll take it."

I placed my hand on the crook of his arm. As we walked, I asked, "You're really not involved with the woman in there?"

He glanced down at me. "Martina and I are business partners. She's had a rougher journey than I have. As far as I know she doesn't have any family, so I share mine with her. She's brilliant, bossy, and a good friend. There never has been and never could be more than that between us."

"Did she get along with your wife?" Yep, I went there.

He gave me a long look as if debating whether or not he would answer my question. "When things were good between Tasha and me, they got along fine. When you run a business with someone, they see you at your best and worst. She didn't think Tasha was good for me and, in retrospect, she was right."

"No one handles losing a loved one well."

His eyes darkened. "We were already having problems before she was killed in action."

"And you feel guilty about that." It wasn't a question because I could see the truth in his expression.

"Remember how I said I was a miserable bastard who

hates everyone? For the past year that has included myself." I felt the deep breath he took before he said, "I'm working on it."

I almost smiled at that.

I gave his arm a squeeze in support. Although I knew next to nothing about him, I couldn't shake the feeling that I already knew all that mattered. We'd both survived something that we were still struggling to put behind us. We'd both kept people at a distance because a part of us was still broken. Could we offer each other anything more than understanding? I didn't know, but as we stepped into the small clothing shop together he didn't feel like a stranger anymore.

I sent a quick text to Lorraine to say I'd gone to a store to buy something clean but that I would be returning soon. He sent off a text as well. Nearly instantly a woman asked us if we required assistance.

I explained that I'd had a small accident and was looking for a simple dress to change into. She hustled me off to a changing room. The dresses she brought me were nice but one was too loose, another too tight. One showed enough cleavage that wearing a bra would have been impossible. The next she brought me buttoned straight up my neck.

From the other side of the door, Benjamin said, "Here, try this one."

I had to open the door a crack to accept his suggestion. It was the same color as the one I'd worn to the restaurant. There were minor differences, but from a distance it could pass for the same dress. And it was in my size. My friends might notice when I walked back in wearing it but no one else would. "It's perfect. Thank you."

Holding my old dress in one hand, I came out of the dressing room wearing my new one. Benjamin smiled. "Beautiful."

I blushed. "It's essentially the same dress."

"Which you also looked wonderful in." When he raised a hand toward me I tensed until I realized he was reaching for a price tag. "You'll want to take this off."

My hand found the tag he'd touched and I gave it a yank until the fastener that had held it to the dress snapped. "Got it."

"That one looks perfect on you," the clerk said as she approached.

"We'll take it," Benjamin said smoothly.

"Absolutely," the woman responded.

He pulled out a credit card and handed it to her.

I waved a hand for him not to. "I can buy the dress."

"Let me do this for you," he growled.

I nodded and just like that I was allowing a man I'd just met to buy clothing for me. Since starting over on my own I'd prided myself on working hard and paying all of my own bills. I didn't like feeling that I owed anyone—not even the men I'd dated.

This was different. Benjamin was hovering somewhere between friendship and the sexiest mistake I'd ever been tempted to make. I didn't want to say no.

He held the door for me as we left the shop. The walk back to the restaurant felt too short. I didn't take his arm again and he didn't ask me to. We stopped just outside the restaurant.

"I want to see you again," he announced.

I searched his face. What did he see in me? I wanted to assure him he'd met me when I wasn't my best. Normally I wasn't a clumsy, emotional wreck. "You have my address. You don't have my number?"

He grimaced. "Is that a trick question?"

I smiled. "Thank you for the dress, Benjamin. If you'd like to call me, I'd like to hear from you."

He leaned in. "And if I also want to taste those sweet lips of yours?"

His grin was so damn sexy I almost did kiss him right then. I made the mistake, however, of checking if anyone from the restaurant could see us. Behind the glass window Lorraine, Emmie, and Keiona were wide-eyed watching us. They waved. I waved back then returned my attention to Benjamin. Feeling younger and happier than I had in a long time, I said playfully, "Then you should definitely call me."

With that I opened the door of the restaurant and slipped inside before he had a chance to say more. His parents and Martina were watching me just as closely. Feeling a little brazen, I waved to them as well.

All three smiled and waved back and my heart started pounding. Amazing how things could be entirely different than how they had appeared. As I took my seat again, Benjamin rejoined his family. Our eyes locked across the room and for a moment there was no one but us and the sizzle of our attraction.

Then he winked.

My face warmed and I looked away. Part of me didn't want our time together to end, but another part of me understood that this wasn't the end.

This was our beginning.

I let out a breath and tucked my wet dress mostly into my purse before stashing it at my feet. The meal I'd ordered arrived as if by magic. I smiled at the waiter, at my friends, then across at Benjamin.

"So, who is Mr. Tall, Dark, and Handsome?" Lorraine asked. "And do we have to run over the woman he's with?"

I laughed. "He's—a friend." For now at least. "And he's not with her."

"Good thing," Emmie said, "or she might be over here trying to pull out your hair. Keiona, do you remember how Leon's date did that at . . ." She snapped her fingers. "Why can't I remember whose wedding that was? The police were called because they took their brawl to the parking lot."

Keiona laughed. "Kenny and Liz's wedding. Oh, yes, that was a doozy. Caterina, have you ever seen a hockey fight?"

"No."

"Well, it was exactly like that except all the referees were in frilly dresses. There wasn't a man there who wanted to get between those two women once the fake nails started flying. Thankfully the police arrived quickly. What a wedding."

Emmie added, "Leon's still single if you're interested."

"Shocking," I said with a smile. "I'm all set."

"She doesn't need our help." Lorraine nodded toward

Benjamin's table. "You don't have to tell us if you don't want to, Caterina. We completely respect your privacy."

Keiona joked, "We'll be slowly dying every single moment you don't tell us, but we won't complain."

"There's not much to tell. I met him the other day. That's it. I didn't expect to see him again." The expectation in their expressions as they waited for more was impossible to hold out against. I leaned in and said, "Okay, he asked me out but I turned him down. Then he sent me a gift—"

I told them about the gift, my reaction to it, where I'd stashed it, as well as his explanation that he hadn't known the messages would be what they were. "He said he just wanted to make me smile."

Emmie brought a hand to her chest. "He likes you! I wish you'd seen him sprint out of here after you. It was adorable."

Basking in the warmth of their friendship, I opened up more and told them how he'd suggested the clothing shop and gone to it with me—as well as how he'd been the one who'd found the perfect dress for me. "I like him too."

With a huge smile Lorraine lifted her phone and took a photo of me as well as him at his table. "I'll send these to you. My husband took me to a fair for our first date. We took photos in one of those little booths that spit out a string of them. I came home and started a scrapbook with those photos. My friends thought I was crazy, but I knew he was the one."

"Then she found out he was still sleeping with his ex," Keiona added.

Lorraine rolled her eyes skyward. "It did take him a few dates to realize what I knew right away."

In a low voice Emmie said, "He fell for her when she found out he was sleeping around and she threatened to tie his testicles around his neck like a bow tie."

Lorraine burst out laughing. "He does actually claim that was when he knew. It was scary/sexy. As if I would ever do such a thing."

"You didn't see her when she found out about the other woman," Keiona said with round eyes as she mimicked tying a bow tie around her own neck. "I would have believed her. The man is only with her because he fears for his manhood."

"Thirty years of fear," Lorraine joked. "And house full of kids. The poor man."

Emmie waved a hand. "He adores her, but I do love that story. Now for me it took longer. Roger says he fell for me the first time he saw me. I was working in a grocery store at the time. He asked me where something was and I thought he was sweet, but maybe not my type. Then he came in the next day and asked me where something else was. Before I knew it, he was coming to see me daily during his lunch shift and I started looking forward to seeing him. We've been together for twenty-eight years and he still asks me where everything is—but I can't complain, I guess, because I knew what I was marrying."

The love in Emmie's eyes when she talked about her husband warmed my heart. I'd given up believing anything like that was possible for me, but what if it was? What if meeting that person didn't have to wait for me to be perfect?

What if I could find someone who could love me the way I was?

I looked across at Benjamin and flushed right down to my toes when our eyes met. Would he come and go as so many had in my life? How did someone know?

Lorraine said, "Keiona, tell her about how you met Terrel."

Keiona shook her head but she was smiling. "You like the story too much."

Emmie leaned in. "Only because Keiona is normally so perfect none of us believed her until Terrel showed up at her door."

Keiona fanned a hand at her face as if to cool herself. "You know when people say what happens in Vegas stays in Vegas? It doesn't. My husband is five years younger than I am, which doesn't sound like much now, but when we met he was eighteen and I was twenty-three. To my credit, I didn't know how young he was."

Smiling, I leaned in as well. "Okay, I do have to hear this."

Emmie chuckled, "It's so good."

Keiona continued, "I'm not the Vegas type. I don't like gambling and I don't drink. But I had a cousin who was getting married and I was in the wedding party. We did a few rounds of shots and I ended up talking to Terrel. Somehow that led to waking up naked in his bed the next morning." She took a breath before continuing, "He was a virgin and so grateful I was mortified. The rest of the weekend he followed me around like a puppy. When I found out how old he was I felt like a cradle robber."

Lorraine chuckled. "Tell her about how he came to see you at the airport."

"Oh my God," Keiona said. "So there I was, hoping I could go home and pretend none of it had happened and he showed up at the airport with his parents to see me off. He told them he was in love and I was the one for him. None of us believed him but it made for a really awkward send-off." She smiled. "I thought he'd forget about me as soon as I was gone, but he asked to come see me in Boston. I almost said no, but he was so sweet. And guess what? The sex was even better sober. After that he flew out to see me once a month—straight through college. As soon as he graduated he told his parents he was moving to the East Coast and marrying me. We shouldn't have worked out. No one thought we would, but he's my best friend and has been since all those phone calls we made in the beginning. I'm the only one he's ever been with. He asked me once if it was the same for me and I said 'Sure.' He didn't ask again."

We laughed with her over that one, especially when she added, "Don't ask questions you don't want to hear the answers to. Besides after being with him for over thirty years I can honestly say I don't remember who I was with before him." She waved a finger at each woman at the table. "My kids don't know the truth about how we met so this is between us. I don't want to have to murder any of you."

Emmie made an X over her heart. "To the grave."

"Your kids are old enough for you to tell them," Lorraine said.

Keiona countered, "I'll tell my kids about how I met Terrel if you tell your kids the testicle bow tie story."

Lorraine picked up her fork and knife and cut into her steak. "So, Caterina, have we scared you off coming out with us?"

I looked around the table slowly. "Not at all. I just hope you'll ask me to do something with you again."

"You hear that, Emmie," Keiona said, "we're still cool."

Emmie chuckled, "Of course we are. No one is more fun than ladies in their fifties. We're young enough to still raise hell and old enough to not give a shit who judges us for it."

Lorraine nodded. "There is a freedom that comes with age. I used to worry about so much when I was younger that just no longer matters to me. I don't even keep grudges anymore. Life is too short."

Keiona took a sip of wine. "I don't miss the angst. Youth is definitely wasted on the young. I spent so much energy trying to change people—or change myself to please other people. Then one day it hit me . . . maybe, just maybe . . . this is me. This is as good as I'm going to get. The best I'll ever look. The healthiest I'll ever be. Everything from here on is downhill so I might as well enjoy the ride."

It was the humor in her voice as she shared that dark image that made me laugh in response. "I'm not quite there yet." I circled my face in the air with one hand. "The angst is strong in this one."

"You should come to yoga with us. Meditation helps," Lorraine said.

Emmie added, "What helps is when Tuesday night's instructor calls in and the class is covered by the martial arts guy. I don't mind stretching for him at all."

Lorraine gasped, "Emmie!"

Emmie shrugged. "I'm married, not dead. If God didn't want us to look he wouldn't send that man to teach our class. I mean if that's what makes it so I can't get into heaven . . ." She sighed. "I'm willing to burn a little."

That had us all laughing again. Still chuckling, I glanced over at Benjamin. A taste of him might just be worth the risk of a burn. As if he'd heard my thoughts he shot me that sexy grin of his.

My heart leapt to my throat, though, when everyone at his table rose to their feet and headed over. "They're coming over."

Just above a whisper, Lorraine said, "Smile. Never let the in-laws see you bleed."

"They're not—"

Benjamin reached the table first. "We're leaving, but I didn't want to without introducing you. Mom, Dad, Martina—this is Caterina."

I stood and shook their hands. It wasn't nearly as traumatic as I would have thought. They were friendly enough and excused themselves soon after being introduced to everyone with me.

"I'll call you," Benjamin said when it was just us left standing beside my table.

"I'd like that."

He took the time to shake the hand of each of the ladies. "It was a pleasure to meet you. I hope to see you again soon."

He gave me one last look, bent until his lips were just above mine, so close I was certain he'd kiss me, then straightened and left. I swear I didn't start breathing again until he'd left the restaurant.

When I sank back into my seat, Emmie said, "Now that's a keeper."

Lorraine added, "How sweet was it that he brought his parents over?"

"I'm glad he introduced you to his business partner. I watched her expression when she shook your hand. She likes you. They're not fucking," Keiona said.

I bit my bottom lip. "But will he actually call?"

Emmie tossed her napkin at me. "The real question is— what are we having for dessert because I'm starting my diet tomorrow so this is my last hurrah."

Keiona shook her head. "I'm not dieting, but I did see the dessert tray and I think we should all order something different and share."

Lorraine tipped her head in my direction. "Are you okay with that? We've been friends for so long that we don't have many boundaries anymore."

Her words shot through me in the most wonderful way. I raised my wineglass and said, "To friendships—old and new. And to desserts so wonderful they're worth sharing."

They all raised glasses and clinked them together. Emmie said, "I'll drink to that."

"Me too," Lorraine and Keiona said in unison.

If there had ever been a more perfect day, I couldn't remember it. It could have been due to the wine or all the sugar, but I smiled the whole ride home.

Chapter Seven

Benjamin

FEELING RESTLESS, I hit the gym at my apartment building after dinner. It didn't take the edge off, nor did the long, cold shower I took afterward. Dressed in only a black prototype pair of boxers from a startup company Martina was considering investing in, I grabbed my phone and a beer and stepped out onto the balcony of my apartment.

I couldn't get Caterina off my mind and not in the usual naked fantasy way.

I hated that someone had hurt her. "Maybe not in the way you're thinking, but yes."

What did that mean? Whatever they had done had been bad enough that she was still struggling with it. I kept going over parts of our conversation.

"I've been in situations where I wasn't in control and—when I feel trapped I panic."

Trapped. Who had made her feel that way? Was Clay's guilt the reason he wanted nothing to do with Caterina? Was he that much of a douche?

Both my parents and Martina had been excited about the

idea that I might have found someone I was interested in, but this didn't feel anything like what I'd felt before. Tasha and I had hit it off instantly, jumped right into bed together, and called it love before either of us knew what the fuck it was. It had been so easy with her. So simple. No arguments. Nothing to overcome. We'd felt perfect for each other—until she'd served me a plate of reality that tore down that illusion.

I took a long drink of my beer then looked down at my phone. The situation with Caterina was so opposite of how it had been with Tasha I couldn't decide if it was better or doomed. I didn't do complicated and that's all this was.

Just thinking about Caterina suffering at the hands of anyone had my stomach tied in knots. I wanted to hold her and promise her that no one would ever hurt her again.

I wanted to call her and demand she tell me what happened to her.

I was tempted to track down Clay and shake the shit out of him until he either told me everything or woke the fuck up and owned up to what he'd done. Caterina obviously still cared about him. I hated that after whatever the hell he had done to her, he hadn't gotten his shit together enough to be there for her when she'd reached out to him.

Like I said—complicated. Caterina needed someone who could guide her through her pain. No one had ever accused me of being the nurturing type. What the hell was I thinking? She probably needed to talk things out. My parents required professional help to realize speaking to each other was important. What did I know about healing anyone?

It wasn't as if Caterina was alone in the world. The women she'd been with seemed to genuinely like her. There was a very good chance she would be fine, even better off, if I never contacted her again.

The problem?

I'd told her I would call and I wanted to.

Tomorrow.

Not tonight. She's probably still out with her friends.

I could send a text to make sure she made it home okay.

I took another swig of beer. This is ridiculous. If I want to send her a text I should just do it. My fingers hesitated above the phone screen then texted: **Checking that you made it home okay.**

Benjamin?

Yes.

It's almost midnight.

I checked the time on my phone. **Shit. Sorry, I didn't realize it was so late.**

No, that's okay. Usually I'd be up, but after all the shopping we did and the wine I had with dinner I guess I was really tired. I fell asleep on the couch in my dress so I should probably thank you.

That made me wish I'd been there to carry her to her bed and tuck her in. I shook my head to clear it of that image. I didn't drink as much I guess because I came home and hit the gym for a couple of hours but I'm still wide awake. And suddenly itchy beneath the cloth of my boxers. What the hell?

Can I call? she wrote.

Absolutely. I answered as soon as her call showed on my

screen. "Hey."

Her voice was delightfully thick from sleep. "I wanted to thank you for how kind you were to me today. Both for coming out to check on me and for the dress."

"You're welcome."

"My friends all thought you were wonderful. I told them about the gift you sent—"

"What the fuck?" Holy shit my dick and balls felt like someone was lighting them on fire. I headed in from the balcony and noted a rash emerging on my bare stomach. "That's not good."

"It's okay they all had equally embarrassing stories about how they'd met their husbands." She gasped. "Not that I'm implying that anything big would happen between us, I'm just saying . . ."

"Hold on." I stripped off my underwear. The rash was everywhere the material had touched. Everywhere. My eyes started to water. "Sorry, I have to go. I'm dealing with something right now."

"Oh. Of course." She sounded so sad it snapped my attention away from my burning crotch and back to her. Not an easy feat.

"Listen, I'll call you again. Soon."

"Don't bother. I thought we had a connection, but—"

"It's not you, it's me. Literally."

"I don't understand you. Why even text me?"

I growled and stomped a foot to attempt to stop the itching. "You don't understand and I sure as hell don't want to explain."

"Wow. Okay. Then good night."

"Wait. What should I take for a rash? Like a quickly spreading all over rash?" My vision was blurring and I wiped at my watering eyes.

"A rash?"

"An all over body one. Benadryl, right?" I waved the phone in the air as I stomped into my bathroom to look through my medicine cabinet. "I don't have any, shit."

"Sounds like an allergic reaction to something."

"Yeah, I got that."

"Send me your address."

I typed it in a text then said, "Normally I'd love to see you, but this isn't a good time. I've got to get in the shower."

"I'm not asking to come over, I'm going to send you something. I know a pharmacy that delivers twenty-four/seven. Go take that shower and by the time you finish it'll probably be there. Take it right away, then stay on the phone with someone. And call nine one one if you have any trouble breathing."

If I hadn't been so itchy that I was going out of my mind I would have been moved by her concern. All I could do though was thank her quickly and hang up as I sprinted toward my bathroom.

What I thought would make me instantly feel better had a completely different affect. I was crawling out of my own skin by the time my doorman announced a package had been delivered. I told him to bring it up and met him in just my towel. His expression when he held out the small paper bag to me said he was afraid to touch me. I understood. It looked as bad as it felt. I snatched the bag, thanked him, and slammed the door.

With water from the sink I downed two pills. Caterina had also sent a tube of Benadryl lotion. I let my towel fall, looked at the sad condition of my genitals, said "Fuck it," and applied it everywhere I could reach.

Sweet relief.

I walked gingerly back to where I'd left my phone. Caterina had told me to stay on the phone with someone and, well, how many people did I really want to know about this? I blew my nose quickly before calling her. "Hey."

"How are you feeling?"

"A little better." I kicked the offending underwear to the corner of the room. "Sorry I was so short with you earlier."

"That's okay. Allergic reactions can be serious."

"This one sure as hell was." I looked down at my lotion covered dick and laughed even though there wasn't much I found funny about the situation. "Next time Martina wants someone to test out a product she's considering investing in, she can find another sucker. Thank you for the quick-thinking package. I had no idea I was allergic to wool."

"Wool? What kind of product were you testing?"

I weighed the potential that she might find humor in the situation versus the hit to my pride I'd take. Deciding I could weather it, I said, "They're supposed to be the next generation of high-tech male underwear. It's an industry that has had a surprising amount of growth. This one claims it is cooling in all weather conditions. Nowhere on it did it mention its ability to set my dick on fire."

She coughed. Coughed again. Then laughed. "Sounds painful."

"It was but I'm standing here wearing about half the bottle of lotion you sent and feeling better."

"Oh, you shouldn't put that much on."

"Trust me, the boys needed it."

She chuckled again. "I'm sorry, that's quite an image you're putting in my head."

I placed one leg up on the edge of my bed to allow more air to where cooling was needed. "Not since my teen years has my dick been this grateful to a woman."

She laughed, but her tone was dry. "I do what I can." A moment later, she added, "I just looked up what to do for a wool allergic reaction and it says not to take a shower. The hot water can make your reaction worse."

"Now you tell me."

"I didn't have all the information earlier or I would have."

As a little inside joke to myself regarding what my parents had just learned, I said, "So communication is key."

"In wool underwear emergencies—apparently."

"You'll be happy to hear the rash is receding."

"That's—that's—I really don't know what to say to that. Congratulations?"

As the intensity of my reaction faded, my ability to think straight returned as well as my sense of humor. "This wasn't how I imagined our first phone conversation going."

"Second. Our first one consisted of more swearing."

I smiled. "Good news? Things can only go up from

here." After a pause, I asked, "Is it too soon to ask if you'd like to see me on Saturday?"

"Too soon?"

"Should I wait until the image of my inflamed manhood fades from your mind first?"

"That won't happen soon." She laughed again. "And I guess it depends how much of yourself you intend to show me."

I laughed at that. "We'll start with the parts I didn't have to lotion tonight."

"Sounds like a good idea. Yes, I'd love to see you Saturday."

I wasn't someone who spoke on the phone often. I was much more comfortable exchanging texts even with women I was intimate with. I wasn't ready to hang up, though. "Should I surprise you or would you like to help me plan the day?"

"No one has ever asked me that before."

"I thought since I don't know you well enough to know which situations make you feel—"

"Thank you." She cut me off before I said something I probably shouldn't have brought back up. I wanted to make her feel comfortable, but my approach was like a bull in a china shop. I tended to be brutally honest. Could she handle it? "I'm not really good at talking about things that bother me. I know, it's my fault because I brought it up, but I wish I hadn't. I wish—"

"Caterina, we all have issues. Trust me, I have plenty of my own. I don't apologize for them, though, because I can't be anyone but who I am."

She was quiet for long enough that I began to wonder if we'd been disconnected. When she spoke again her voice was thick with emotion. "It has been a rough week. I wish this wasn't how we'd met, but I can't be anyone but who I am either."

"You don't have to be." If I could have crawled my lotioned ass through the phone line and hugged her I would have. "Just be honest. Where do you want this to go?"

She sniffed. "I need someone in my corner. God, that sounds pathetic. But you asked. Yes, I'd like to date you, maybe even sleep with you, but if you really want to know what I need—it's someone I can rely on. Just one person I can trust."

Her words shook me to the core. Her pain was so raw, so real, I sank to sit on the edge of my bed. No matter what happened between us, I knew I would never be the same. "I want to be that person."

She sniffed again. "You don't know me well enough to mean that."

"And you don't know me well at all if you think I say anything I don't mean."

She cleared her throat. "How are you still interested in seeing me? I'm not normally so . . . so . . ."

To lessen the tension, I joked, "I would never ditch a woman who sent Benadryl for my boys. That shows real heart."

She chuckled and sighed. "Or something."

"Listen, no one has ever accused me of being too nice,

but I've always been someone people could rely on. Even when things get ugly. Even against someone others would be afraid to take on." I needed her to know Clay and all his money didn't scare me.

"My biggest fight now is with myself. I've chosen to be alone for so long I've started to think it's all I can be. But I want more than I've allowed myself."

"I've worked seven days a week since my wife died. I'd started to believe that was all I could be as well. I don't know what we'll end up being to each other. Maybe this is the start of something or maybe we'll just be a sounding board for each other. There's no way to know unless we give it a try. All I'm sure of is that I want to see you again."

"I want to see you too." She added, "And I'm glad your manhood didn't burn off."

That had me smiling again. "You had to go there, didn't you?"

She chuckled. "Sorry. It was impossible to resist."

Just like she was. "Go to bed. We'll talk tomorrow."

"Benjamin?"

"Yes?"

"Surprise me with what we do for our date. I need to be okay with surprises."

Her trust in me was something I didn't take lightly. When she ended the call, I lay back on my bed, closed my eyes and threw an arm over my face. She needed a friend more than she needed a lover.

Could I be that for her? Did I want to be?

She made me ache in so many ways.

Caterina Landon, what the hell kind of first date do I plan for you?

I was still asking myself that same question the next morning when I walked into my office. Instead of getting to work, I pulled a chair up to my PA's desk. "Harami, I have a question."

Her smile was polite but I could tell my unusual behavior had her concerned. "I may have an answer."

"What would you imagine is the least threatening first date a man could plan?"

She took a moment to answer. "I would think that would depend on the woman you're planning it for. Tell me something about her."

I rubbed a hand over my chin and thought back to the reason Caterina had been at the Landon Foundation the day we'd met. "She's brave but you can tell she has gone through some tough times. She told me she doesn't like to be anywhere she can't leave because she has been places she couldn't."

Harami nodded slowly. "I understand now. You have a kind heart, Mr. Drover."

I let out a breath audibly and gripped my knees. "I don't know about that, but I do want to do this right."

"Then you will. Have faith that it will work out and it will."

"That has not been my experience."

She looked down at the photo of her husband on her desk. "Faith is strongest when it is tested and survives." When she looked up there was more wisdom than sadness in her gaze. "You're the same. You were tested and you survived. Whoever this woman is, she's lucky she's meeting you now when you're stronger, kinder, better able to understand whatever she suffered. What you've been through can be one of your greatest strengths if you let it be."

I nodded toward the photo of her husband. "How is he?"

"Proud. Stubborn. Always doing so much more than the doctors suggest. He drives me crazy with this, but I drive him crazy with all my worrying. He says when it's his turn to go to the crematorium, I will be there making sure the oven is not too hot, nor too cold, or too drafty." Her smile was strained. "He's probably right."

I leaned forward and placed my hand briefly on hers in support. I'd always be there if she needed me to and she knew that. I stood and joked, "Well, thank you for giving me absolutely no helpful advice."

She chuckled. "Anytime, Mr. Drover."

I started to walk away then stopped and turned back toward her. "This woman is different. I can't explain why, but she is."

"Then plan a date that is as different as she is and she will love it."

Harami's suggestion echoed in my thoughts long after I went into my office and closed the door. Plan something as different as she is.

I did an internet search of the best unusual outings in Massachusetts and scrolled through pages and pages of them until I found one that made me smile.

Unique.

Somewhat ridiculous.

Interesting.

Perfect.

Chapter Eight

Caterina

SATURDAY MORNING AS I drove to the address Benjamin had sent me the night before, I let myself get excited. I didn't do anything like this normally. Although he hadn't told me what we would be doing on our date, he did suggest I wear casual clothing—something I'd be comfortable walking outdoors in. He also asked me not to look up what was in the area or his surprise would be ruined.

Had he picked me up and driven me to an unknown location my anxiety would have been unmanageable, but by asking me to meet him there he'd given me what I needed—an escape route. My GPS announced I was arriving at my destination. The sign at the end of a driveway read, "Cranberry Stables." I pulled in and parked in a spot next to where he was already waiting beside his car.

After taking a fortifying deep breath, I opened the door of my car and stepped out. He walked over to greet me.

"You made it."

I swallowed hard. God, he was even better looking than I remembered. He'd looked good in a suit, but jeans accentuated his muscular thighs. His gray T-shirt wasn't tight, but it hugged his chest in a way that made me want to run my hands over the expanse of it. When our eyes met I struggled for what to say that wouldn't reveal how affected I was. "I did."

He smiled and my breath caught in my throat. "I'm glad. Have you ridden horses before?"

I wanted to say yes. In theory I had no fear of large animals, but I hadn't spent time around them. "No."

"Would you like to?"

"Oh." I looked around at a rider in a ring who rode like she had been born on a horse. My hands became cold and sweaty. "Like that?"

"No, I booked a trail ride. When I spoke to the owner he assured me he had horses that are so calm anyone's grandmother would feel comfortable on them." He made a face. "Not that I think you're—"

"Sounds perfect." It was my turn to smile.

He looked relieved. "It's a short ride, more like a tour of where we will be going next."

I searched his face as a thought occurred to me. "You put real thought into this."

His eyes darkened. "I heard you. If there is any part of today that you're not comfortable with, just say so. Although I am looking forward to the cookies at the end so I'd prefer you agree to at least that."

His level of consideration was truly touching. "How could I say no to cookies?"

"Exactly." He motioned with his head toward the barn's

office. "Ready?"

There was an awkwardness to how we walked side by side into the office—together, but not touching. Happy to be with each other but not yet comfortable. We signed a few forms then were led back outside where three horses were saddled up and waiting for us.

A tall, lanky teenage girl introduced herself as our guide. Along with the man who had signed us in, she led the horses to a mounting block. "First up," she said, "Biscuit. He's a Tennessee Walker so he'll be a nice smooth ride. You don't have to know how to ride at all to enjoy him. He'll just follow along. Best part? He's as lazy as they come. If you're not asking him to go anywhere he'd rather just stand. Which one of you is the one who wanted the calmer horse?"

"Me," I squeaked. Even though she'd told me he would be good, I worried that my nervous energy would affect him. I stepped forward and touched his neck softly.

The horse turned his head and sniffed my ear. I made myself stand still for it, but my heart was racing and I was certain he would bite my head off.

"He likes you," the girl said.

"Good boy," I said tentatively, giving his neck another pat.

"We don't have to do this," Benjamin said gently from beside me.

I shot him a smile. "I want to." I did. Part of breaking out of the slump I was in involved pushing myself out of my comfort zone. This was as out as I could imagine. I stepped up onto the mounting block and followed the instructions on how to get on the horse.

As directed, I gave his sides a little squeeze so he would walk off, but as soon as I released my legs he stopped walking. I gave him another pat. "Good boy, Biscuit."

Next the girl brought a white horse to the mounting block. "This is Skye. He belongs to my dad. He's a Missouri Foxtrotter. Super calm, but sometimes he dances a little when he is asked to wait."

Benjamin took the reins from the girl and gave the horse a pat. "I used to ride when I was younger. It's been a while, but I'm sure I'll be fine." He got on the horse with a confidence I envied and moved the horse away from the mounting block to stand beside mine.

"You good?" he asked.

Biscuit yawned beneath me and I chuckled. "Yes. I don't think Biscuit has any desire to run off."

"Nor do I."

It was an odd thing to say, but also really nice to hear. I quickly looked away as I realized I felt the same way. "That's good because you're stuck with me at least until the cookies."

"Ready?" the girl asked from atop her own horse. "The cranberry bog is this way."

"Cranberry bog?" I asked.

"That's the real surprise," Benjamin said as he and his horse began to follow behind the girl on her horse.

I had to ask Biscuit to go or he likely would have stayed behind and napped. Once he was plodding after the other two, I said, "I knew there were bogs in Massachusetts, but I've never been to one. I hope we'll have time to look around."

"I'm sure we will," he answered.

For the next half hour, we rode the dirt roads as the young girl told us about the history of the cranberry bog that had been in her family for six generations. Cranberry growing was family farming at its best, with most of the local bogs owned by families for multiple generations. These farms still produced the majority of the cranberries used by large commercial sellers. Cranberry vines were tended and passed down like heirlooms. Some vines in the area were more than 150 years old and still bearing fruit.

The bogs themselves were stunning. Large rectangular strips of water were bright red from the floating berries. "You've come at the right time," the girl said. "We're harvesting so we have filled the beds with water. This is my favorite time of year."

"Why do you add the water?" I asked.

"The berries are all still on the vines," she answered, "but they have air pockets in them so they float even on the vine. We use harvest tractors like that one." She pointed to a machine with a long spinning roller in front of it that was moving across the water. "The spindle on the front of it agitates vines enough that they release the berries which then float to the surface and can be gathered. We use a boom which is a floating containment device that gathers all the berries together so we can pull them to shore. That's what they're doing over there. Want to try it?"

My eyes rounded. "Try it?"

Benjamin turned partly around in his saddle. "We'd have

to wear waders, but harvesting cranberries sounds fun."

I looked around at the small groups of people standing in water that was about mid-thigh high surrounded by the floating red berries. They were all smiling and helping in different ways. Some were moving the berries with what looked like rakes. Some were helping to pull the boom that encircled a large area of floating berries. It did look fun. "I'd love to."

We rode to an area where we dismounted and handed our horses off. Then Benjamin and I each stepped into ridiculously large waders. Mine came up to my armpits. His closer to his waist. They had straps that came over our shoulders like overalls and another strap that secured it around our waists. I would have felt foolish if Benjamin didn't look just as silly.

He stepped closer and leaned down to say, "Well, this confirms it, you look good in whatever you wear."

I blushed. "Sure." He'd only said it to be kind, but when he looked at me that way I felt beautiful.

A young man joined us. "Ready to jump in and help? There's no time to waste in the cranberry business. We have about six weeks to harvest about a hundred acres of berries. If you were here a few weeks ago everything was dry. Berries don't grow submerged under water. As soon as we flood the bog the race is on." He looked at Benjamin. "You look strong. Follow me, I'll teach you how to corral the berries by pulling the boom in smaller and smaller circles." He looked at me. "I'll give you a rake and show you how to push the berries toward the hose that will suck them up, clean them off, and sort them. If you do a good enough job, Stan might let you take a ride on the beater. Nothing like driving through the bog on it. It's like a cranberry Zamboni."

Before he led us into the water, he showed us berries that were still on the vine and floating. At his urging, we each picked one and tasted it. I made a face. "Tart."

Benjamin's expression mirrored how I felt. "Not bad, but I can see why people don't eat them like strawberries."

The man nodded for us to follow him and said, "It's the tannin. If you've ever eaten a banana before it's ripe and gotten that mouth drying taste, it's the same chemical. Cranberries might not taste good ripe, but they are a super-food. Whether it's treating UTIs, cardiovascular health, improving oral hygiene, or battling cancer . . . cranberries pack a lot of good in tiny little floating packages."

"I had no idea," I said and touched Benjamin's arm. "This is really interesting. Thanks."

He placed his hand over mine and simply smiled down at me. "I'm glad you're enjoying it."

"I am." There was heat in that simple touch that rocked through me. There we were, both covered in huge waders, with a young man looking on and waiting, and I wished I could stretch that moment into a lifetime. In that place, beneath the warmth of his gaze, I wasn't angry anymore. Nothing scared me. Anything and everything felt possible.

"Caterina?" he asked in a husky tone.

"Yes?" I flicked my tongue across my bottom lip.

"Someone is trying to hand you a rake."

"Oh." I had to shake my head to clear it and laughed only to cover my embarrassment.

An older man held out a wooden tool to me. "Time to work," he said.

"Of course." I took the rake and reluctantly followed him a short way away from Benjamin. Once inside a circle of cranberries, I tried to listen to the instructions the man was giving me, but I couldn't look away from Benjamin. As he hauled what looked like a large black ribbon through the water behind him, his muscles flexed and bulged. So strong, but not full of himself as I would have thought. He appeared to be genuinely listening and taking the task seriously.

Me? I had no idea what I was supposed to do with the rake so I just kind of swished it around in the water while sneaking look after look at Benjamin.

"I'll never hire you to harvest cranberries," the man beside me said.

"I already have a job," I answered without looking away from the sight of Benjamin laughing at something the man beside him said.

"My wife doesn't enjoy harvesting either, but she sure can bake. I hear the two of you are going to learn to make her famous cran-orange cookies later."

"I'm looking forward to it." I nodded and clutched the rake to my chest. Benjamin had planned the perfect first date, one so wonderful I didn't know what to do with how it made me feel.

"If it wasn't crunch time in harvest season I would let you just stand there, but do you see all the cranberries around you? Try to get at least a few of them over to that hose."

Benjamin glanced my way and I raised the rake to move the berries in the correct direction. The smile he shot me warmed down to my rubber boot covered toes.

A few minutes later, the man beside me whistled for one of the other men to take us out on the beater. As Benjamin rejoined me, he offered me his hand. I took it and nothing had ever felt so right. We waded through the water to where a machine paused to wait for us. It was a large machine with a spinning part in front and a pronged rake behind. There was a place on the side for us to stand and hold on to a railing. After greeting us, the driver explained that he needs to stay on a specific path and go in the correct direction or the machine will pull up the plants. If the water wasn't there, he explained, we'd be able to see which direction the plants lay in. He'd take us for a few swipes across the bog then drop us off at shore. After that his mother was waiting for us back at the house to give us a baking lesson.

"Is everyone here a member of your family?" Benjamin asked.

The man looked around. "About half. We bring in extra hands during harvest time. But, essentially this is a family business. My children are already working in the store. We all enjoy it. As soon as I was old enough to walk I was following my dad around the bog. It's in our blood."

I tried and failed to imagine what it would be like to be that attached to a place or that much a part of a family. I thought about all the people who thought money would solve their problems and how wrong they were. This—this was worth more than any dollar amount. Would I ever feel so connected to anyone or anything?

When the man restarted the tractor, it jolted forward, and Benjamin stepped closer and used his body to steady mine. He raised his voice to speak over the sound of the tractor's engine. "What are you thinking?"

I tensed when his arm went around me and almost moved away, but forced myself to relax. It wasn't like I hadn't dated anyone, but everything with Benjamin felt like . . . more. It was so good I had trouble believing it was real. I also didn't want to put up the usual barriers I hid behind. And that scared me. "This wouldn't be such a bad life." I wasn't referring to just the farm.

His arm tightened around my waist. "It's nothing like how I grew up, but I agree."

Tipping my head back so I could see his face, I said, "Your parents seemed like very nice people."

"Oh, they are. I don't have any complaints about my childhood. They ran a successful business that kept them busy, but I was well cared for and they gave me the skills to be successful in my own right. I wouldn't be where I am today without their guidance."

"That's great." Only it wasn't. It was obvious we had very different opinions of what success was. Money didn't matter to me at all. I turned my face away to hide my disappointment.

He bent his head closer. "Then why did you say that like I just admitted to something illegal?"

"Did I?" I met his gaze again. What could I say that was

the truth without opening a door to topics I didn't want to discuss? He already knew Clay was my brother. He must know I'd been born wealthy. "We all choose our own paths. I chose a simple one."

"As opposed to?"

I tensed against him. How honest should I be with him? "It's great that you're doing so well."

He frowned. "But?"

I wasn't able to meet his gaze when I said, "In my experience wealthy people place more importance on money than people."

"So, to be a good person I'd have to struggle financially?"

"I didn't say that." I shifted more away from him. "Could we change the subject?" My chest tightened despite my attempts to calm myself. The last thing I wanted to do was ruin the date. The tractor turned, sending me stumbling against his chest. He steadied me, but this time didn't put an arm around me. I hated that I was the reason.

We didn't say anything for the next pass across the bog and soon enough the ride was over. Benjamin and I hopped off and made our way to shore, returned our waders and were met by a young man who said he would take us up to the house for a baking lesson.

On our way, Benjamin said, "Would you rather end the date now?"

I didn't want that at all. For longer than I could remember I had kept people at a distance, kept my defenses secure and in place. And where had that gotten me? I needed to do better. "No. Benjamin, please don't let me run you off."

He stopped walking and turned to me. I stopped as well. For a long moment he searched my face. A door to the house we had been walking toward opened and a middle-aged woman in an apron waved to us from the door.

"Caterina and Benjamin?" she asked.

"That's us," Benjamin answered while looking down into my eyes. Us. He glanced toward the door then back at me. "Caterina—" He bent toward me and brushed his lips gently across mine. Time stopped for one glorious, charged moment. I swayed against him.

It would have been too easy to forget we had an audience. Kissing him felt too right. I broke off the kiss and stepped back.

He didn't look happy, but he said, "I'm not going anywhere."

I wanted to believe him.

Chapter Nine

Benjamin

MOMENTS LATER, I was sporting a white apron and feeling oddly at peace despite how unfamiliar I was with such a setting. In front of us there was a variety of bowls with ingredients in them. I was irritated with myself for kissing Caterina in pubic and putting her in an uncomfortable position. It was difficult to think straight when I was around her.

To Caterina, the woman said, "My name is Francine, but you can call me Frannie."

"My name is Caterina—people call me . . . Caterina."

If I hadn't been standing so close to Caterina I might have thought she was trying to keep things formal, but I was beginning to be able to read her. She was nervous.

"Thank you for having us, Frannie. You're welcome to call me Benjamin." I winked at Caterina hoping the little joke helped ease her discomfort.

Frannie looked us both over. "Is this your first cooking lesson?"

"And our first date," Caterina blurted out then went delightfully red.

I smiled when she met my gaze then looked away.

"And I get to be a part of it," Frannie said graciously. She lifted a bowl of berries. "I hope you come back and share that you've gone off and made these many times for each other. These are not just cranberries—they're over a hundred years of work by this family. They're love, loss, grit, and laughter. The recipe I'm going to teach you is the one my husband's grandmother taught me when I married him. Some people are very protective about their family's recipes, but here at the Cranberry Stables at the Bog, we believe that recipes are like love—better when they are given generously and freely."

Caterina was all eyes. "That's beautiful."

Just as I had sensed her pain, I could feel Caterina's yearning as if it were my own. I took her hand in mine. "I wouldn't wear an apron for just anyone."

She smiled up at me. "It suits you."

"Does it?" I joked back. There was a lot I could have said, but not in front of Frannie. For that reason alone, I tore my gaze from Caterina and said, "Our visit to the bog has been amazing so far. Warning, I'm coming in with high expectations."

Frannie laughed. "I'll do my best to not disappoint." Without hesitation she began to explain the recipe ingredients to us. Caterina and I took turns combining and mixing the ingredients.

There was a comfortable rhythm to it that had us both relaxing and smiling. When the dough was balled and placed on parchment-paper-lined cookie sheets, Frannie announced, "Now for my secret ingredient."

Caterina and I exchanged a look.

"Wine."

"You put wine in your cookies?" Caterina asked.

Frannie laughed. "Oh, no, but it helps pass the wait for the cookies to bake." She pulled out three glasses and a bottle of tawny port. At our nods of agreement, she half-filled each glass then raised hers. "To first dates, new friends, and possibilities."

That was something I was willing to raise my glass to. Caterina clinked hers to Frannie's, then to mine, before taking a sip. Caterina's smile was impossible to look away from. "Thank you, Frannie. This has been wonderful."

She waved off Caterina's gratitude. "Why don't you two go sit at the table on the side porch. I'll bring a plate of cookies to you when they're done."

I thanked Frannie as well then, wine in one hand, walked with Caterina to the porch. After holding out her chair for her to sit, I took a seat across from her. "That was actually more fun than I expected."

Holding my gaze, Caterina said, "It really was." She sipped her wine. "I'm going to fall into bed after this." Her mouth rounded. "My bed. Alone. I just meant that it has been quite a day."

"Got it." Her awkwardness would have been adorable if I didn't know it stemmed from real uncertainty. "I like you, Caterina Landon."

She blinked a few times quickly, looking so serious I

wanted to hug her, but held back. She said she was looking for someone she could trust and that would take time—for both of us. In a husky voice, she said, "I like you too."

"What do you think about sharing another adventure next weekend?"

Her smile started small then spread across her face. "I would like that."

I raised my glass. "To second dates, new friends, and possibilities."

She raised hers as well and tapped it to mine. After taking a sip, she placed her glass down. "Seriously, this is the nicest date I've been on—possibly ever."

I did and didn't like to hear that. "Then you've been with the wrong men."

"I don't date much. I don't like to lie and usually as soon as someone starts getting close to me they ask about my past—my family." Her expression tightened. "I shouldn't have been so upset when I heard that Clay denied my existence. Whenever I've been asked, I've denied any relation to him. I had to, though, for my safety."

That made sense. "Perhaps he denied you for the same reason."

She shook her head. "No. Clay doesn't care about me enough to be concerned about what happens to me."

I reached out and took her hand in mine. I hated that she was likely correct. "You don't have to tell me what happened, but if you need to talk it out, I'm here." As the words came out of my mouth I realized how being with Caterina was already changing me. I'd spent the last year thinking about me—my pain, my anger, my loss. It was past time to change that.

She was quiet for a moment, then said, "Thank you. I feel the same way about you and your wife."

"I have no desire to talk about her." I hadn't meant for my tone to be as abrupt as it was. Old habits were tough to put aside.

She gave my hand a light squeeze. "I get that. I can't imagine anything I enjoy talking about less than my family. It's just refreshing to be with someone I don't have to lie to."

Outside of our attraction, that was another lure of Caterina . . . I felt like myself again . . . my old self. Seeing a light at the end of the tunnel made the darkness of the journey through it less oppressive. "I've spent the last year telling everyone I'm okay, but I'm not. Not yet, anyway. I'm still angry. Usually talking about it only makes it worse."

"If you replaced last year with 'for the last decade' I'd say that's a good description of how I've been doing."

Our connection in that moment was so strong I downed the rest of my wine in one gulp. Anger wasn't how I felt then. My heart was racing. I'd probably smiled more that day than I had over the entire last year. "I've hardly gone anywhere because I felt like there was nothing outside of work for me."

She nodded. "I've made sure I've never worked too long in one place because I didn't want to get attached to anyone. The women you saw me with the other night are the only friends I have and that was the first time I agreed to go out with them."

"I drank heavily for a while after Tasha died."

"I got into drugs after my brother died."

"Every time someone tells me they understand, all I want to do is punch them in the face. I don't, but I want to."

Her smile was empathetic. "In the beginning I wanted to do the same to everyone who said what happened to me couldn't have been as bad as I thought it was."

Sharing felt more natural with Caterina than it ever had with anyone—even Tasha. "Before I met you I was broken in a way I didn't want to fix."

Her hand shook beneath mine. "I don't know if I'm ready for this."

"I sure as hell am not, but that doesn't mean I don't want it to happen."

She brought her free hand up to her mouth and her eyes filled with tears. "There's a saying that if everyone around you is an asshole it's probably not them, it's you. Every time I count on someone they let me down. What if it's not them? What if I'm bringing this on myself and don't see it?"

I give her hand a little shake. "Hey. I told you I'd be what you need me to be. You said you need someone in your corner, one person you can trust. I'm known for being brutally honest. If you need a reality check, I'll give it to you."

She laughed and laced her fingers through mine. "Oh, really? And if I see you feeling sorry for yourself I might just kick your ass."

"Good."

"I tend to pull away when I get scared."

"I bark when cornered, but I don't bite." I grinned after that one and only because I couldn't resist, I added, "Unless I'm asked to."

She chuckled, then let out a shaky breath. "I miss my brothers. I want to let go of the past, but even when I try to do better I can't."

"My parents are driving me crazy trying to make up for all the nurturing they didn't have time for until they retired. Martina is loving it. I'm doing my best to be okay with our new normal."

"When I saw you with Martina in the restaurant I did think you were a couple."

"I'm not her type," I said with humor. "Nor is she mine. I do love her, though. She and I have been through a lot together." I told Caterina more about how we'd met and how that had become a work partnership. I left out what didn't need to be shared, but did say that I was currently reaping what I'd sown as far as encouraging Martina to speak up for herself.

"Mr. Drover, I do believe I have misjudged you. You're a big softy under all that growl."

"I wouldn't say that, but I do think the world would be a better place if people stepped forward now and then to protect those in need."

Her smile faded. "I don't need saving."

I brought her hand up to my lips. "We all do. I've been a miserable bastard. You've got your work cut out with me."

The corners of her mouth twitched before her smile returned. "I'm up to the challenge."

"So am I."

Frannie appeared and delivered a plate of cookies. After placing it on our table, she paused and clasped her hands above her heart. "The two of you remind me so much of how my husband and I were in the beginning. Is it wrong that I'm imagining you returning year after year with your children?"

I froze.

Caterina's eyes rounded.

Frannie laughed. "Well, now that I've scared you both right out of that second date, enjoy your cookies."

I was barely breathing when I met Caterina's gaze. Once upon a time a wife and kids had been part of my life plan, but that was BT. Caterina and I might help each other heal, have a good amount of sex along the way, but more than that? I'd closed the door on trusting anyone to that level again.

To second dates, new friends, and new possibilities.

What was planning to see Caterina opening the door to? Was that really what I wanted?

Caterina looked away and downed the rest of her wine. Keeping her eyes averted, she said, "The cookies look delicious."

Cookies?

What cookies?

Chapter Ten

Caterina

TOO SOON WE were standing beside my car. The date was over and it was time to say good-bye. I wasn't ready to. "Benjamin, thank you for planning all of this."

"Come here."

I don't know a woman who would not have obeyed that husky command. I stepped closer and tipped my head back so I could see his face.

"I don't want your gratitude." He brought a hand up and brushed a thumb across my lips. "I want this." His mouth claimed mine. I shifted closer, running my hands up his solid chest. He wrapped his arms around my back, enveloping me in his essence. As our kiss deepened I forgot we weren't alone in the parking lot. Every place our bodies touched burned deliciously and made me want more.

I opened my mouth to his skilled tongue and passion seared through me. To an onlooker it might have appeared a rather chaste kiss. Our hands didn't wander. Our clothing stayed in place. However, there was nothing chaste about how my body revved for his. There had been other men, but none that had ever fanned this kind of need in me.

I'd learned to be careful, tread lightly, go slowly. I'd learned to keep a part of myself separate from even those I had sex with. A quick exit had always been top priority.

When Benjamin kissed me, my fears fell away. I would have followed him anywhere, promised anything just to continue to feel as good as I did in his arms. It was scary, but the kind of scary that is also so exciting you don't want it to end.

Did it have to? I had my own car. We could go back to his place and take this where we both wanted it to go. I moaned and melted against him.

He tightened his arms around me and did the most delightful, skillful things with his tongue that I imagined burying my hands in his hair while his tongue danced lower, much lower. There was no doubt in my mind that he would be amazing at that as well.

I clung to him when he lifted his head. For a moment there was only our ragged breathing and each other. If the fire in his eyes was anything to go by he was about to ask me to go home with him.

Hell yes.

Show me the way.

His voice was gravelly when he said, "So, next Saturday."

I bit my bottom lip lightly. "Or sooner." Like now.

Anywhere you suggest.

With significantly less clothing.

He ran a hand through my hair and sighed. "I have a busy week, but I'll call you."

What?

Was I sending mixed signals? Did he need more clarity? I writhed my body against his. "I don't have plans for tonight." If he needed clearer than that I might as well hold up a sign saying, "Please fuck me."

His head bent closer and my eyes began to close again. Yes.

"I don't mind taking this slow." He gently set me back from him.

My hands flew to my waist, I frowned up at him and I almost gave in to a good, old-fashioned foot stomp. "I've never slept with a man on a first date."

"That was my guess."

"And I wasn't implying I would sleep with you tonight."

"I understand."

My hands fisted at my sides. "Forget it." I was lying, but I was embarrassed. I'd never thrown myself at a man before. I certainly wasn't expecting one to turn me down flat if I did.

"Caterina?"

I took a deep breath. "What?"

"It's not that I don't want to."

"It doesn't matter because it's not happening." If I could have snapped my fingers and disappeared I would have. "I should go. This was a mistake."

He reached out and gently took hold of one of my arms. "Look at me."

I couldn't. I was too angry—with him, with myself. "Don't touch me."

His hand dropped away. "If you were any other woman

this date would have probably ended with sex."

I rolled my eyes and shook my head. Was that supposed to make me feel better? It didn't.

He stepped closer. "You're not the first woman I've dated since Tasha. I don't even remember the names of some of them. That's not what I want with you."

I raised my eyes to meet his gaze.

He continued, "I'm not in a good place, Caterina. I have shit to work out. So do you. I don't want to fuck and forget. For the first time in a long time I felt like my old self and it was so damn good. I want more of that."

My heart started thudding wildly in my chest. Hugging my arms around myself, I said, "I'm just embarrassed."

His tone was gentle. "You shouldn't be. Not wanting today to end means I did something right."

I looked for any hint that he didn't mean what he was saying, but there was only warmth in his expression. He liked me. No games. No pressure. No man had ever made me feel so exposed yet so safe at the same time. To ease some of the tension of the moment, I said, "You shouldn't kiss like that if you're not going to put out."

He laughed. "I'll keep that in mind." He held out a hand toward me. I hesitated then put my hand in his. He pulled me to his chest and tucked me under his chin. "I don't know if I'm doing this right, Caterina, but it feels too important to rush."

I wrapped my arms around his waist, buried my face in his chest and did the least sexy thing I could think of—I burst into tears. He rocked his body back and forth to comfort me. This. This was that I'd never had. I cried for the damaged child in me. I cried for the lonely woman I'd become. I cried because everything I'd spent a lifetime yearning for was right there in the safety of his embrace.

When I finally calmed, I sniffed a few times and brought a hand up to wipe the tears off my cheeks. "I'm sorry, I don't know what that was about." I sniffed again. "I wouldn't blame you if you didn't actually call after today."

With a hand that cupped my chin, he tipped my face up toward his. "I don't know what happened to you, Caterina, but you're not alone anymore. I'm right here and I'm not going anywhere."

I let out a shaky breath and searched his face. "So, Saturday?"

He hugged me to him. "Absolutely. Would you like to plan that date?"

The day had been an emotional roller coaster. What I really wanted to do was stay where I was forever, but that wasn't possible. I raised my head. "I would."

Chapter Eleven

Benjamin

I TOLD MYSELF to give Caterina a little space leading up to our next date, but ended up pacing from room to room in my apartment until I called her. She sounded cautious when she answered, "Hi, Benjamin."

"Home safe and sound?"

"Sure am." She cleared her throat. "About how our date ended—"

"If you're about to apologize, don't." Female tears were normally something that made me slightly uncomfortable, but hers had gutted me. Her pain wasn't that of someone who was frustrated or had their feelings hurt. It was from a real trauma that she was still battling the effects from.

"I just want you to know I don't end every date in tears."

"Caterina, I don't know who made you feel like you're not an incredible woman that any man would be lucky to land a second date with, but I had a wonderful time with you." Deciding it was best to change the subject, I did. "So, where are you taking me next weekend?"

"I wasn't planning—Are you still okay with meeting me

instead of us driving over together?"

That she had to ask meant we still had a way to go before she knew me well enough to trust me. "Of course."

She made a relieved sound. "I was thinking we should go to Salem."

I hadn't taken her for someone who would enjoy a haunted tour, but if that's what she wanted, I was in. "Sounds interesting."

"Have you ever been?"

"A long time ago. I went with some friends on Halloween."

"I feel like there is so much more to the town than that. I haven't been, but I've done some reading about Salem's history and it's fascinating. The town I'm working for has a few descendants from those who lived through the witch trials. I didn't find any first-person accounts, but there were some journal entries from people who recorded stories their family passed down from generation to generation. It was interesting. I'd love to see how the museum compares to what I read."

I sat down on my couch and took a moment to soak in not only her suggestion but her enthusiasm on the historical subject. Many of the women I knew would have suggested we go somewhere where they could see and be seen by movers and shakers in Boston. In my social circle I either brought the arm candy or I was it. I thought back to what Tasha and I had done together and the list was surprisingly short. Dinner. Sex. Parties. Parents. Repeat.

It was a pattern that I hadn't questioned. In terms of relationships, I'd always considered myself more like my father than my mother, but being with Caterina was forcing me to reevaluate that. My mother had been raised to behave by a clear set of norms. I might not have been groomed to be a socialite, but I was only then becoming aware of the low expectations I had when it came to partners. I didn't expect them to be intellectually stimulating. I didn't require that we shared any of the same interests. We didn't even need to connect on any deep emotional level.

No wonder Tasha had found it so easy to walk away from a marriage with me.

Had I taken the time to be her friend first I wouldn't have been side-swiped by her desire to be a Marine. I would have known what was in her heart.

Caterina wasn't telling me she wanted more from me, she was showing me. Like my mother, I was being given an opportunity to step up.

"Salem sounds really interesting. I'm in for however you plan out our time there."

Her tone turned less sure. "It doesn't sound all that romantic. Your date was so upbeat. I'll think of something better."

"Caterina, you could say our second date will be a tour of a back alley and I'd enjoy it. It's about seeing you and not about where that happens."

After a moment, she said, "So you've got a thing for alleys."

I laughed. "Yes, that's what I'm saying."

She sighed. "Salem probably isn't a good idea. When I

read the journals of the descendants, they were inspirational—stories of survival and perseverance. Most people don't focus on that aspect. The people who were accused, jailed, suffered but survived to piece their lives and their families together wouldn't sell tickets or make a blockbuster movie. History focuses on those who were convicted and died, but there are so many more stories of both men and women who spoke out against the trials and for that reason alone were persecuted." Her voice became thick with emotion. "Three centuries later, as recent as 2001, the convicted were still being exonerated which is good, I suppose. It was because of what they suffered that our legal system changed to allow the cross-examination of accusers as well as the presumption that one is innocent until proven guilty. So, good comes out of even the worst situations, I guess. That's what I need to believe anyway."

The way she identified with the victims of that time had me piecing together everything she'd told me about what had happened to her. She'd been somewhere she couldn't get away from. Something horrific had happened to her there. Her brother had been involved. Had Clay accused her of something? Had she spent time in jail?

There was a time not so long ago when I would have told her that we had all survived something and that pain was just a part of life. Suck it up. That wasn't what she needed to hear and it wasn't what I necessarily believed anymore. She was looking for something that until I'd met her I hadn't had myself—hope.

I cleared my throat. "Without realizing it, I had fallen

into a dark place where I forgot that although we can't change what has already happened, we do have control over how we spend our present and future. I let the past have too strong of a hold over me. I was angry all the time about something I had no way of changing and that kept me stuck in that place."

"Until?"

"Until you."

She gasped. "You mean that."

"I do." As we spoke an idea came to me. "So, let's go to Salem. Let's face what happened to those people, but before we leave let's come up with something we can do for the ones who have been forgotten. Let's give them a voice."

"I hate you," she said with a sniff. "You're going to make me cry and I do not want to break down in front of you again."

Chest tight, my own emotions running high, I said, "You're not breaking down, you're healing. It might not show as much on me, but being with you has shaken me up in the best way also. I feel like I'm coming back online, waking up after a long slumber. This is important to you, but it's important to me as well."

Neither of us said anything for long moment. "So, Salem."

I smiled as I repeated, "Salem."

"I'll find something to do that day that will surprise you as well."

I could have said every single moment with her had already done that. "I look forward to it. I'll call you tomorrow morning. I have a feeling that any day that starts with hearing your voice will be a good one."

"Is that what you say to all the ladies?" she joked.

"Never." It was true. Not even with Tasha. That realization made me a little sad. For as much as she'd disappointed me, I was beginning to see that I had likely disappointed her as well. "Good night, Caterina."

"Good night, Benjamin."

Long after the call ended, I sat there on my couch, letting the enormity of the day wash over me. There was a time when I might have avoided that level of emotional involvement. I wasn't that man anymore. What would that mean moving forward? I wasn't yet sure, but I knew I didn't want to go back.

Caterina's tears didn't scare me, they healed me—challenged me to do better this time. When I thought back to the arguments I'd had with Tasha when she'd told me she was deploying, I felt ashamed. I never once asked her why she'd wanted to see battle so badly or how I could support her better.

It had felt like a betrayal because I had looked at all of it in terms of what I wanted, what I needed. I'd accused her of not honoring our marriage vows, but I hadn't either.

I thought about the day I'd gone to see Clay. I'd made that about myself as well. I could have put my irritation aside and played nice. If I had, her final wish would already have been fulfilled.

Tasha.

I have no idea if you can hear me, but I'm sorry it took

me so long to wake up.

You deserved better.

I don't know why donating your inheritance to the Landon Foundation was so important to you, but I'll make it happen.

You probably think I'm not the right man for Caterina. I might not be, but she's broken just like our marriage was. I can't do anything about how you and I let each other down, but I can be there for her. I can learn from what you and I did and didn't do.

I felt a little sick when I remembered how everyone had turned against Tasha when she'd left for the Marines. Her family as well as mine had judged her harshly. We'd all aligned against her. Even when she'd died none of us had celebrated her sacrifice. We'd mourned her, but we'd selfishly viewed her death in terms of how it had affected us.

This time, I'm listening, Tasha. I'm going to ask the questions I should have asked you. I'm going to be the man Caterina needs, the one I should have been when you needed someone on your side.

I stood and walked to my bedroom closet. From beneath other boxes, I dug out one I had stashed away soon after receiving it. I carried it back to the living room, placed it on my coffee table and pulled out a triangular wooden and glass display case.

Etched into the glass was Captain Tasha Drover, followed by the dates of her birth and death. In the bottom left corner of the case there was a photo of her in uniform. In the bottom right—was her Purple Heart as well as several campaign ribbons. Behind them was the flag that had been draped over her coffin. As I touched the front of the glass I remembered asking her parents if they wouldn't prefer to keep the case at their home. Even though her mother had ordered the shadow box, both she and Tasha's father had said that was not how they wanted to remember their daughter.

It took me until that very moment to understand the gravity of what they'd meant. They hadn't wanted to remember Tasha for who she was—only who they'd wanted her to be.

I removed knickknacks that some decorator had thought my apartment's fireplace mantel required and replaced them with Tasha's shadow box. She and I might not have been a good match, but she would be remembered for the hero she was and not the person anyone else thought she should have been.

I'd thought moving forward required forgetting, but I understood then that healing came from the opposite. I'd hated Tasha for leaving me, but someone like her was probably haunting the shit out of the people she loved—keeping us safe.

Tasha, I believe you can hear me. I'll get your money to the Landon Foundation and the families you want it to help, but there's something I need you to do for me.

Watch over Caterina. And don't let me mess this up.

Kick my ass if you have to. I smiled. We both know you probably could.

In my head I heard her laugh and it was a freeing sound.

My step was lighter as I left my living room and stripped down for bed. That night I had the best sleep I'd had in years.

Chapter Twelve

Caterina

A T THE TOWN hall the next morning, I sat at a table full of photos and journals that needed archiving, but my thoughts were far away from the musty records' room. I was still smiling from my brief conversation with Benjamin. He'd called just to tell me he hoped I would have a good day and that he was thinking about me.

Swoon.

He was thoughtful and attentive. I kept waiting for him to give me a reason not to trust that this could be real. Every time I thought I couldn't like him more he said or did something that made me sad I'd ever settled for less.

"Well, don't you look happy," Lorraine said as she placed another box of papers on my table. "The date with Benjamin must have gone well."

I propped my chin up on one hand and let out a happy sigh. "It was perfect."

Pulling up a chair beside me, she said, "Don't tell me anything I can't tell Keiona and Emmie. I'm meeting them for lunch today and you know they'll grill me." She tipped her head to one side. "You should join us."

"I'd love to." It wasn't the first invitation to lunch I'd received from them, but it was the first one I didn't hesitate to agree to.

Lorraine bit her lip and stood. "I should wait until then to hear about the date—that way you don't have to say it all twice." She made a pained face and sat back down. "I can't wait until then." She slapped a hand down on the table. "No, I need to be strong." Then she laughed. "How about if I call them and we all go for a coffee now?"

I laughed while shaking my head. "I wouldn't want to bother them."

"Bother?" She took out her phone and sent a text. A moment later she said, "They're on their way. Did you have breakfast yet? What is coffee without a little something to wash it down?" Another text came in and Lorraine smiled. "Emmie said her favorite donut flavor just came into season so she'll start her diet tomorrow."

When Lorraine stood I did as well. I grabbed my purse. "Does tomorrow ever come?"

We began walking to the door. "For her I hope it doesn't. She's just a few pounds over, but she went on a strict diet several years back and it was not fun. That woman does better with a little sugar now and then."

"So do I." I held back a laugh when Keiona and Emmie pulled up in a car almost as soon as we reached the front door of the building. "Wow, that was fast."

"They were probably already on their way. When I spoke to Emmie this morning I joked that I'd get the most detailed version of your date because you know how people begin to simplify the more times they tell people something." She chuckled. "I'm sure she called Keiona and told her what I said."

As we approached the car Keiona lowered her window. "Don't you dare say another word, Caterina. Save it for when we can all hear."

Feeling like I'd fallen into an alternate universe, one in which I had friends and a regular social life, I slid into the backseat of the car. "It's not nearly as exciting as you probably think."

Emmie turned in her seat. "We'll be the judge of that."

Lorraine touched my arm. "Remember, anything you say can and will be brought up again and again probably until the day we all die. If it's juicy enough, who knows, we might find a way to put it on your tombstone. Keep that in mind as you choose what to share."

"I will." I laughed again. These ladies were hilarious.

Keiona shook her head. "Lorraine, don't scare her into holding back. Caterina, did that hunk wake up at your house?"

"W-wake up?"

Emmie pulled the car back out into traffic. "It sounds safe to assume your date was PG-rated, which means we don't have to stay in the car to hear it. So hold off until I get a coffee in my hand."

I winked at Lorraine. "I don't know, it was a great date. Can you wait that long to hear about it?"

"What are you implying?" Emmie shot me a smile in the

rearview mirror. "You're still a young thing, but when you're old like us, you'll realize the importance of celebrating all the good stuff."

"Old?" Keiona scoffed. "Speak for yourself. I'm fifty-five years young."

Before there was time for a good rebuttal, we were pulling into the parking lot of the local donut shop. We hustled inside, found a nice table near a window, and put in an order for coffee all around and some donuts.

Once it was delivered, Emmie clasped her coffee mug between both hands and said, "Okay, Caterina, spill. Where did he take you?"

I told them about how I'd met him at Cranberry Stables and about how we'd started our date with a trail ride around the bog.

"That's so romantic," Emmie said. "Roger and I used to do stuff like that. Well, maybe not like that exactly. He used to take me fishing a lot. We did have sex near that lake in Sommerville, though. And that was romantic. Except for the time I got poison ivy."

"Focus, Emmie," Lorraine said with a chuckle. "This is about Caterina."

"Oh, yes. Sorry, Caterina."

I was quickly falling in love with these women. "That's okay, Emmie. Hang on to that poison ivy story, because I want to hear it right after this."

Emmie's smile shone. "Poison ivy is definitely better than head lice. Lorraine and Ted decided to role play once so they rented these Victorian outfits from a costume place . . .

wigs and all . . . and they both got head lice."

Lorraine threw a napkin at Emmie. "See what I mean, Caterina? Share one X-rated, head lice story with this crew and you'll never hear the end of it."

Keiona scratched delicately at her scalp and shuddered. "You couldn't pay me enough to wear someone else's wig."

Lorraine nodded. "In retrospect it wasn't a good idea." Her smile returned. "The sex the costumes inspired, though, was worth it. It's good to shake it up now and then."

My face flushed, but I was grinning. "Where have you ladies been all my life?"

"Right here," Emmie said as if it had been a real question. "I thought about moving away once, but everyone I love is here."

I couldn't remember what it was like to feel that way. There must have been a time when I did—when I was young, but those years were blurred to me.

Keiona waved a hand. "Could we get back to why we came? So you went on a trail ride. Was that it?"

I shook my head then told them about the waders we'd put on to "work" in the bog and how handsome Benjamin had looked even in that outfit. I felt a little giddy as I described the baking lesson followed by sipping wine on the porch of the owner's home. "It was the perfect first date."

I left off the part where I'd wrapped up the date with a good ole cry. I wasn't ready to share that with anyone, especially since mentioning that would introduce the topic of me not being in the best mental place, and that wasn't how I wanted these women to see me. I was letting down my walls, but it was a process. "But now I have a problem."

"You do?" Lorraine leaned in, concerned.

Without missing a beat, I said, "I'm planning our next date and he has set the bar high. I want to plan something just as memorable."

"Show up naked," Emmie joked.

Lorraine rolled her eyes. "Emmie!"

Emmie threw her hands up in the air. "Ask any man and he'll say that would be the kind of memory he'd treasure."

"Oh, Lord," Keiona said with amusement.

Hand on one hip, Emmie challenged Keiona. "Say I'm wrong. Say it, but no one will believe you."

"She's right," Keiona conceded. "But I do think you could do better for your second date."

I wrinkled my nose. "Just a little. Okay, let me tell you what I have planned so far." I put my coffee down. "Oh, and what he suggested we do while we're there. You could actually help with that part. Before I look into anything seriously, I'd like to know if there is interest from this community."

"Now I'm intrigued," Lorraine said.

"We're in," Emmie promised.

Keiona joked, "I'll wait until I hear what group activity you're hoping people will be interested in before I agree to anything. I'm not as wild as I used to be."

We all laughed at that one. I rushed to explain. "Nothing like that. I thought we'd go to Salem to the museum. The witch trials have always fascinated me, even more so now that I've read journal entries about that time period from descendants who relocated to this town. I told him I'd been thinking about all the people who were affected but were forgotten by history and he suggested that while we're there we see if we can find a way to commemorate them. It doesn't have to be anything huge. A plaque or a bench or something. I thought it would be nice if we mentioned the names of those we know of who are ancestors of the people here. Maybe we could do a similar plaque here that mentions the one in Salem."

The table fell silent for a moment.

Lorraine was the first to speak. "That would be beautiful. I'll ask around, but I'm sure we could raise funds for it."

I shook my head. "I can donate it. I have some money saved and this is something I'd really like to do for the town."

Keiona brought a hand to her chest. "What an amazing thing to do. Now I feel bad about the orgy joke."

"Like I said," Emmie interjected, "we're in."

Lorraine snapped her fingers. "Don't we know someone at the Salem Historical Society? Lizabeth? No. Linette . . . Alvia's aunt. I'm sure she would love to sit down with you and get that project started."

Emmie groaned. "I'm sure Caterina doesn't want her second date with beautiful Benjamin to include time with Alvia's aunt." She leaned toward me and stage whispered, "That woman talks so much she'll never die—God would lose patience with her and the Devil couldn't top her stories."

Keiona nodded. "She is a talker. The trick is to go to see

her around two o'clock. Her daughter calls her every day at two thirty. She'd walk away from giving someone CPR to take her call."

"That's the truth," Lorraine said.

"I'll keep that in mind." I took a bite of my donut to give myself a moment to consider what Benjamin would think of meeting Linette. It definitely wasn't the sexiest thing I could imagine planning, but he did seem to want to take it slowly. "See if she'll meet us—at two." I nodded in thanks to Keiona.

I said, "I need something unique to do after that. I really enjoyed the bog, and it was obvious he'd put a lot of thought into making the date special for me. What could I do that he's probably never done before?"

The four of us took a few minutes to consider our options. When they started sharing, I took notes on my phone, but none really jumped out at me.

Finally, Emmie said, "Are you okay with a little bit of a drive? I have a cousin in New Hampshire who is a little . . . eccentric? He bought a hundred acres up there and cleared a large area of it for his hobby. He doesn't usually let anyone outside of the family onto his land, but he adores me and I bet he'd do this for me."

"Since we'd be done with Salem by two thirty, I guess we'd have time to drive somewhere. Especially if it's something you think Benjamin would enjoy."

"I don't know a man who wouldn't," Emmie said with confidence.

"Oh, boy," Lorraine said, "are you referring to your

cousin Harry?"

"Yes, and you can't tell me we didn't all have fun when we went up to see him."

"We did," Lorraine said with less certainty than I would have liked. "But does Caterina really want to risk her man throwing his back out before they get down to business?"

Keiona rolled her eyes. "Benjamin is in his prime. If he can't handle being jostled around a little, sex with him won't be worth it anyway."

I laughed. Screw being cautious. It was time to grab life by the balls and go for it. "I'm intrigued, and more than a little scared, but I think I want to do whatever this is."

Emmie leaned over and gave me a hug. "And that's why you fit in perfectly with us."

Chapter Thirteen

Benjamin

Late Saturday afternoon Caterina and I were on our way up to New Hampshire after spending the first part of the day in Salem. I was driving with one hand because my other was linked with hers. I normally would have said I didn't care where we were headed, but she was so excited about this secret of hers that I was excited about it as well.

I tried to remember the last time I had gone into anything as blind as I was going into this. I wasn't big on trust, but I didn't have a single doubt about the woman next to me. We'd spoken twice a day since our first date.

Crazy.

Unbelievable.

And yet it felt right.

I liked starting my day with a little bit of her.

Even more, I enjoyed ending my day talking about everything and anything with her. I shouldn't brag, but by the end of the first week I could have taught a class on the history of the people in the town she was cataloguing. I felt like I knew Lorraine, Keiona, and Emmie personally.

Surprisingly enough, Caterina could probably have said the same about not only my family, my employees, but also my childhood friends. For someone who didn't enjoy talking all that much, I found myself sharing all kinds of stories with Caterina.

Looking back, I was probably sharing that much with her in an attempt to get her to open up to me. There was only so far back she was willing to discuss. She told me about her college friends and the jobs she'd worked since. If I asked about anything before that she shut down.

Having seen the fallout of her attempt to reconnect with Clay I understood that family wasn't something she was comfortable discussing. I wanted to know, but only when she was ready to tell me.

I definitely didn't want to do anything to remove the smile she'd had on her face since we'd met in Salem. I knew that simply driving to New Hampshire in the same car was a big deal.

She gave my hand a little squeeze. "What was your favorite part of today?"

"Outside of being with you?"

"I'm serious."

"So am I." I glance at her, realized she was waiting for more, and said, "The museum was interesting. A little sensationalized. I guess my favorite part was how excited Linette was to see the journals you brought. I could feel the passion she has for keeping history alive and when you showed her how her husband's family was related to one of the names that will be on the plaque, I thought she would hyperventilate."

Caterina's smile widened. "Lorraine helped me map his family back. I hoped there would be a connection to her, but I think she was just as happy with what we did find."

I raised her hand to my lips and gave it a quick kiss. "She was. She probably wouldn't have stopped talking about it if her daughter hadn't called."

Caterina laughed. "Oh, I forgot to tell you that her daughter calls daily at the same time and that was why we chose that time to meet."

"Genius."

"We can thank Keiona for that tip."

"I'll remember to do that." Caterina had chosen her friends well.

"Emmie is the one who set up today. If it goes as well as I hope it does we'll have to call her on the way home to thank her."

"I love how excited you are about this."

Caterina looked a little embarrassed by my comment. "I haven't planned a surprise for anyone in . . . I don't know if I ever have. I wonder if this is how it feels to throw a birthday party for someone."

"You've never done that?" I regretted the question as soon as I uttered it. Her expression closed up. Her smile remained but was strained.

"How much time do we have before we get there?"

I glanced down at the GPS. She could have read it as easily as I did, but I understood the purpose of her question. "Five minutes."

She nodded. After a moment she asked, "How does the upcoming week look for you? Just as busy?"

She was seeking idle conversation, but I took advantage of the subject of it. "Actually, it won't be nearly as packed. What do you think about grabbing lunch a couple times together? I can come to you one day. Then you could meet me at my office building another day. Harami would love to meet you."

"Harami?"

"My PA. I may have mentioned you to her."

A real smile returned to Caterina's face. "I may have mentioned you to one or two people as well."

If someone had told me that I could get warm and goofy over a woman, I wouldn't have believed them. Caterina was showing me sides of myself I hadn't known I had. For example, when the GPS announced we were nearing our destination I felt another wave of excitement. "Caterina."

"Yes."

"Thank you for this."

"You don't even know what it is."

"Doesn't matter. My heart is racing. I feel like a kid running down the steps to open presents on Christmas morning. I haven't felt anything like this in years."

She gave my hand another squeeze. "I hope you like it."

I turned onto a long dirt driveway after a dented mailbox. There were no business signs, no hint of what she might have planned. Of course, ideas whirled in my head. Everything from a hot-air balloon ride to river rafting. I wasn't dressed for the latter, but the jeans I'd worn would survive just about anything. Maybe a secluded tent where we would take things faster than I'd planned.

The driveway opened up to a larger dirt area with a trailer on one side and a garage that looked large enough to park a Boeing 747 in on the other side. "Is this the right place?"

Her eyes were wide and worried. "I think so."

An older man in jean overalls stepped out of a door of the garage. His hands were covered with grease that he wiped on a rag as he approached. "Is that the person we're meeting?"

"Only one way to find out," she said as she released my hand and stepped out of the car. Her voice was an octave above normal when she asked, "Harry?"

"That's me." The man shot us a wide mostly toothless grin.

I went to Caterina's side. "Benjamin Drover."

He shook my hand. I did my best not to reveal that I wasn't keen on the residual oil his handshake left behind.

"Caterina Landon." Caterina shook his hand as well. If she felt the same, she didn't give a sign. "Thank you so much for having us."

"A friend of the family is practically family in my mind," Harry said. "You ready for your lesson?"

Caterina leaned closer to him and said, "Just so you know, I haven't told Benjamin what we're doing here today."

Harry cackled. "Well, let's go blow his mind."

"You ready, Benjamin?" The sexy challenge in Caterina's smile was enough to have me follow her anywhere—no questions asked.

"Absolutely."

Harry pressed a button on a remote and one of the large garage doors rolled upward. "I'm actually looking forward to this. As my family gets older I don't have as many people to share my passion with."

He flipped on a light and motioned toward two trucks that were jacked up on wheels that were at least five feet high. The height of the truck cabs towered well above ten feet. One was neon green, the other neon orange, both with fire decals on the sides.

I nearly pissed myself. "Are those fucking monster trucks?"

"Yep," Harry said. "Meet Trixie and Tina. They're the reason I don't have a house. Also, more than likely, the reason I don't have a wife, either. These babies don't come cheap."

Caterina choked on a laugh.

My mouth was hanging open. As a child I'd once asked my father if he would take me to a monster truck event. He'd refused. Such events, he'd explained, were for the mindless masses.

"I imagine they don't." I walked up to the truck named Trixie and touched her reverently. Consider me a mindless mass of holy-shit-this-is-awesome. "Do you drive them in shows?"

"I used to, but I retired. Now I just ride them around the course I made for them out back."

"I'd love to see that," I said.

"See it?" He gave me an odd look. "You're here to learn

how to drive one."

I don't know if a man can have an orgasm from something that is completely nonsexual, but the intensity of the adrenaline rush that followed Harry's announcement felt almost as good as one. "Are you serious?" I turned to Caterina, pulled her to me, and swung her around. "He's going to let me drive one."

"I know," she said as she laughed and clung to my shoulders. "That was the surprise."

I hugged her to me. I would have kissed her but I didn't want to make my new best friend Harry uncomfortable. "You have to drive one too."

She tensed and shook her head. "Oh, no. I couldn't."

"Come on, you'd love it."

Still shaking her head, she said, "I wouldn't."

I turned to Harry. "You'd be okay with teaching her as well, wouldn't you?"

"Sure."

"That's settled then. You have to at least try it," I said. Who wouldn't want to?

She tore herself out of my arms and snapped, "I said no. No. When I say no, I mean it. No one has the right to make me do anything I don't want to."

My mood crashed back to earth. "Caterina, no one was going to force you. I just thought—"

"No, what you did was not hear me when I said I didn't want to do it." She was visibly shaking as she looked back and forth between me and Harry. "I'm sorry. I want to leave."

"You just got here," Harry said.

Caterina began to back away. "I'm sorry. I didn't think this through."

I stepped toward Caterina. She took another step back.

"Hang on," Harry said. "I've got something that might help." He walked away.

"Caterina, talk to me." I stopped advancing and lowered my voice. "Nothing has changed since we got here. I was excited, that's all. I'd never let anyone, me or anyone else, force you to do anything. Look at me, I'm the same man you spent the day with. There's nothing here to be afraid of."

She blinked a few times and her eyes started to fill with tears. "I-I—"

Harry returned with a large sledgehammer and handed it to Caterina. She accepted it more out of shock than anything else. "Follow me."

Caterina looked at me. I shrugged. "You're the one with the sledgehammer. I'll go wherever you say." It was meant to be a joke, but she didn't laugh.

After a moment, she turned and followed Harry back out of the garage. He was already a good distance ahead of us in a grassy field. I fell into step beside Caterina. I wanted to say something but didn't know what would make the situation better so I stayed quiet.

Harry came to a stop beside a half-buried car. He waved to Caterina to join him. Now, in my opinion, that scene held more potential danger than driving a monster truck, but Caterina approached him, clutching that sledgehammer like she might use it on him.

Tasha, if you're here, this is where I could use a little intervention. No one kills anyone. No one gets buried in the trunk of that car. We all leave here with the limbs we came with.

Harry turned and pointed to the car. "I got this at the junkyard when I heard you were coming." Yeah, that's not spine chilling. "Emmie told me all the nice stuff you've been doing for the town. I grew up there and this is my way of saying thank you." He looked down at Caterina. "You ever smash a car window with a sledgehammer?"

"No," she said in a slightly wild voice.

"Nothing like it. No better way to let out a little rage, either. When I was younger I left home. Thought I knew everything. I ran with a rough crowd for a while. You know what happens when you play with fire? You get burned. I got burned real good a few times. It gave me a rage." He touched his chest. "Right here. Most of the time I can keep it in, but when I can't I come out here with that sledgehammer and break something. Try it."

She held out the sledgehammer to hand back to him. "I couldn't."

"You'll feel better."

She shook her head. "I'm sure I wouldn't."

He squinted his eyes. "The trick is to imagine the face of whoever hurt you. Picture it right behind that glass and give it a good old crack."

Her chin raised. Her shoulders squared. "I've got a little rage, but I keep it in."

"Let it out," Harry said. He handed her a pair of protective glasses. "Let it out here where no one will judge you and we understand."

Caterina's eyes met mine before she put the glasses on. I couldn't say I understood how she felt because I didn't know what had happened to her, but I understood how denying something only gave it room to fester. "No one needs to ever know."

She raised the sledgehammer over her head and brought it down on the side window but not with enough force to break it. I would have done it for her, but this was something she needed to do. She glanced at Harry who gave her a nod of encouragement and took a better swing.

The window shattered and she let out an audible breath.

"Take out the back one," Harry said.

She took another swing and took the back window out with a powerful swipe. "How about the other side?" she asked.

"Go for it." Harry stepped away.

Glass shattered all around the car, inside and out. Caterina broke the front windshield, the headlights, and the rear window as well. When she calmed, her forehead shone with sweat and her eyes were a little wild, but she wasn't afraid anymore.

She handed the sledgehammer back to Harry. "Thank you. You're right. That did help."

My heart was bursting with both pride in her and an ache that I couldn't erase her pain. All I could do was be there for her. And wait.

She walked over to me, at first keeping her eyes averted.

"I'm sorry."

I reached out and took her hand. "Me too. I shouldn't have pushed you."

Her eyes raised to mine. "You didn't do anything wrong. It's me."

"You can always tell me when you don't feel comfortable." She nodded without speaking so I added, "Just promise me you won't ever do that to my car."

She chuckled and sniffed. "Considering I've never done anything like that in my life, that's an easy promise." She glanced back at the smashed car. "It did feel good, though."

Harry said, "Now imagine how good it'll feel to drive over it. Remember, though, to go over it with your foot on the gas. If you try to take it slow your front tires will hit first and you won't enjoy that experience. Driving a monster truck isn't for the meek, nor is life—not if you're living it right."

She looked back toward the garage then met my gaze again. "I do want to live it right. I don't want to go through life afraid. I hate that I shut down and run. I want to be stronger than that."

I pulled her a little closer to me. "You're not alone anymore, Caterina. When you want to run, know that I'll sprint right along with you if you want me to."

Harry made a grunt of a sound. "That's fucking beautiful, but do you two want to drive monster trucks or not?"

I searched Caterina's face. Sure, learning to drive one would be cool, but what mattered was what was in the eyes of the woman I was already falling for. If she wanted to go, we'd go.

"I'm a shitty driver," Caterina joked to Harry.

"That actually works here," Harry parried back.

Caterina's fingers clenched on mine so tightly the tips of my fingers went numb. "Do you want to try it, Benjamin?"

"Only if you do. I have no problem just driving back to Salem. Your call."

Caterina took a deep breath, closed her eyes briefly, then turned to address Harry. "Okay, let's do this."

"Alright," Harry said. "Once we get you strapped in I'll give you the whole safety talk, but before we get even that far there is something I have to warn you about."

Now I was concerned. "What is that?"

"You're going to enjoy it so much, you'll be asking to come back to do it again and again. It's fucking addictive."

Caterina and I exchanged a look. I said, "That's a risk we're willing to take."

We started following Harry back to the garage when he said, "And of course you could get killed doing it. Blah. Blah. Blah. All you have to do is look at those machines to know they could mess you up more than you could ever mess them up."

"You sure know how to sell the experience," Caterina said with a nervous laugh.

Harry shrugged. "I never died doing it." He spun and smiled at both of us. "I lose a tooth now and then when I'm not paying attention, but I'm still here."

Oh, boy.

Tasha, you might want to bring in reinforcements. We're

going to need a battalion of guardian angels to survive this.

Once inside the garage, Harry gave us each a helmet. "It won't really do shit for you if you fuck up, but it makes people feel better."

Caterina and I exchanged another look, burst out laughing, then put our helmets on. I wasn't a praying man, but I said a few as Harry walked us through how to drive the truck as well as where to go on the course.

"You okay?" I asked when Harry went to get something.

She grimaced. "Just hoping I don't get head lice."

Fuck. I hadn't thought of that.

Chapter Fourteen

Caterina

I WAS A mass of quivering Jell-O when I sank into the passenger seat of Benjamin's car an hour later. One hour. Not one inch of me felt the same. I went to seat belt myself in and started laughing because I doubted any car ride would ever scare me again.

"Are you okay?" Benjamin asked as he slid into the driver's seat.

I nodded slowly. My hands shook as I secured my seat belt. "That was—intense."

He turned in his seat to fully face me. "Are you glad you did it?"

I had to think about that one. "Yes. I think." I ran my tongue over my teeth. "I'm leaving intact, so that's something."

He chuckled. "I feel ninety years old. I pulled muscles I didn't know I had."

Yes. "I'm not sure I'll ever be able to walk again."

"I did catch you smiling a few times."

"Harry was right, once I stopped being so careful it

stopped being painful." I shook my head. "Is that a meta-phor for my life?"

He ran a hand down my arm. "Harry's a good guy, but I don't believe he's an oracle. We all hold back sometimes. What's important is that we don't let it become all that we are."

"I did enjoy driving over the car and hearing it crunch beneath the truck." I made a surprised sound. "I also enjoyed smashing in the car's windows. If either of those had been part of therapy perhaps I would have stayed with it."

The silence that followed my last comment gave me plenty of time to wish I'd kept that last part to myself. I wasn't used to being so real with anyone. After my earlier meltdown it was shocking he wasn't rushing to get me home and out of his car.

His hand sought out mine. "Caterina." He let out an audible breath. "I'm not good at this. In my family we didn't talk about feelings or work through issues. I don't know what you need me to say, but I care enough that I want to say something. Tell me what you need to hear."

He meant it. He wasn't looking for a way out. He was looking for a way in. My breath caught in my throat and although it was an emotional moment I refused to let the tears come. I turned my hand beneath his and intertwined my fingers with his. "You don't have to say anything. Just staying with me is more than I've ever had."

His hand tightened on mine. "What happened to you?"

A knock on his window made us both jump. For a mo-ment I'd forgotten that we were still in Harry's driveway.

Benjamin rolled down his window.

"Car trouble?" Harry asked.

"No, sorry," Benjamin answered. "Just talking before we hit the road."

Harry bent and looked at me through Benjamin's window. "Just checking that I didn't break either of you. You did more than most do their first time out."

It could have been the concern in his eyes or the gratitude that I already felt toward Benjamin, but I released my seat belt, opened my car door, and wobbled my way over to Harry. "I've always been afraid to let my rage out. I thought I would lose control if I ever did. I got burned too. Real bad. I've tried to talk it out, I've tried to pretend it didn't happen. Today was the first time I felt stronger than what happened to me. Facing it was as scary as driving your trucks, but I did both. Thank you." I wrapped my arms around his waist and gave him a long, tight hug.

He gave my back an awkward pat before hugging me back. "You and your man are welcome here anytime. I know good people when I see them."

Benjamin was out of the car again. When I stepped back from hugging Harry, he shook his hand. "You gave us both a day we'll never forget. Thank you."

"Go on," Harry said. "Get out of here. I don't even like people all that much. I've got a beer waiting for me."

Benjamin and I thanked Harry one last time, then got in the car and pulled out onto the road again. Neither of us said anything for what seemed like an eternity. With a couple of hours of driving before us, I knew I had to say something. "If

I tell you what happened to me, it'll make it real again."

He reached out for my hand. "It's already real, Caterina."

I shook my head. "I don't want it to be."

After a pause, he said, "I heard what you said to Harry. You are stronger than whatever happened to you."

I glanced away then back. "How can you believe that after you've seen me panic? No matter how much I piece my life together, no matter how strong I think I've become, it only takes the right trigger and a part of my brain shuts off. In that moment I'm back—I'm back—I can't separate the past from the present. All I know is I need to get away. That's why I always take my own car."

"You trusted me enough to come in mine."

I let out a shaky breath. "I'm forcing myself to push past my fears."

"You can talk to me."

Part of me wanted to, but another part was too afraid of how it might change how he saw me. "You think I'm this sweet, pure woman . . ."

"No, I think you're a good person who had something bad happen to her. I care about you, Caterina. There's nothing you could tell me that would change that."

"What if that's not true?" I had to ask.

His lips pressed together briefly, then he said, "If you're a serial killer that's a game changer."

I laughed a little at that. "I'm not that."

"Are you cruel to children? Do you trip old people on purpose? Steal from the needy?"

"No. I can honestly say I've never done any of that."

"Then I stand by what I said. When you're ready to tell me, I'll be ready to hear your story. I'll also be ready to show you that whatever you think is so bad that it'll change how I see you—won't."

I watched the trees go by outside the window in a blur, wishing I could leave parts of myself behind as easily. He was right, though. I couldn't. No matter how I'd tried to be someone else, the person I saw in the mirror each morning was still me.

"It's a long story."

"We have a long drive."

I thought back to the very first day we'd met. Even before he knew me, Benjamin had waited to make sure I would be okay. If anyone had the potential of seeing the real me and staying, it was him. "My parents had four children. Clay, Collin, me, and Cooper. They died in a helicopter crash when I was six. Clay went to live with our grandparents in England. Collin, Cooper, and I went to live with my father's brother in California. My parents had been wealthy, but nothing like our grandparents on my father's side. They were old money, like so old no one really knew how much they had. They set us up in a big house. I remember fancy cars, lots of house staff. What I don't remember is ever seeing them. Clay either."

My stomach churned as memories flooded back. "As soon as we were old enough, my uncle separated the three of us and sent us off to boarding schools. He didn't pick us up for the holidays. Didn't celebrate our birthdays. I tried to stay in touch with Collin and Cooper but we didn't have much in common after a while. I even reached out to Clay a few times, but he never called me back. My uncle tried to get him to come see us, but all Clay cared about was our grandparents and the money he'd inherit from them."

"I'm so sorry."

"In my teens I decided to take charge of my own life and my relationships with my brothers. I started sneaking away from my school to visit Collin and Cooper. It wasn't easy, but it was worth it. We started to feel like a family again. Sometimes I got in trouble for disappearing. Sometimes the administrators felt sorry enough for me that they didn't record my absences. I didn't reach out to Clay. Relationships go both ways. He never tried to contact me. That said all I needed to know."

I gave myself a moment before continuing the story. As I spoke I needed to clear my throat several times. "Collin was eighteen when he invited me to a party at his school. I went even though I was sixteen at the time. We were both drinking. He slipped away with some friends. When he returned he was out of it—tripping on something. I didn't know a lot about drugs back then. He said he was tired. He went up to his dorm room and fell asleep." My hand shook beneath Benjamin's. "He never woke up."

"Oh my God."

"I felt so guilty about what had happened and so alone. Clay and my grandmother came to the United States. I said some hateful things to Clay. By then he didn't feel like a brother anymore. He felt like some villain in a movie. I hated him. And I guess he hated me because he couldn't leave the country fast enough after Collin's funeral."

"Where was your uncle?"

"He had a big fight with my grandmother. He said he'd asked her to take us back to England with her but she'd refused. She didn't want us any more than he did."

"He said that?"

"He did."

"What a bastard."

"I wasn't right after that. I started doing drugs, getting in real trouble. I'm pretty sure I was hoping I'd die like Collin did."

Benjamin took an exit off the highway and pulled into the parking lot of a restaurant. "Anyone would have felt the same."

"That's not what my uncle thought. He contacted my grandmother. Clay was twenty-two by then. Apparently, she encouraged him to send for me and Cooper, but he refused. Instead, he arranged for me to 'rehab' at Cleaven Hills."

"I've never heard of it."

"Most people haven't. Only the children of the richest families are sent there. It doesn't have an address because it doesn't exist on any government's radar."

"I don't understand."

"Their methods are . . . not legal. The world's most powerful people can't have unruly children but children who are used to always getting their own way can be difficult to break. Cleaven Hills is all about breaking." I glanced at Benjamin's face but had to look away because he looked horrified and now that I'd started to tell my story I couldn't stop. "Clay arranged for them to 'fix' me. I saw the paper-work with his signature. He not only had them kidnap me right off my boarding school campus, but he left me in their 'care' for over a year."

Benjamin's free hand clenched into a fist.

"It was a mobile prison. We were moved from city to city by private plane. Drugged when we weren't obedient. No phone. Strip searched daily to make sure we weren't hiding anything from them. In the beginning I was scared and angry. After a while I didn't feel anything. One of the counselors started having sex with me. It didn't matter that I didn't want to. Nothing I felt mattered. I didn't even want to die anymore. I felt nothing."

He undid his seat belt and leaned closer, putting his head against mine. For once I wasn't crying, but that wasn't necessarily a good thing. Right then, the past had me firmly in its grasp. "They released me when I turned eighteen with a warning that if I ever told anyone about them they would come for me again. I told my therapist that my fear stemmed from being raped, but I didn't tell her how many times or by whom. A part of me is still afraid they'll one day come for me again."

When I dared to look at Benjamin again there were tears running down his cheeks. He was crying the tears I couldn't and I fell in love with him in that moment. His voice was thick when he said, "No one will ever hurt you again, Caterina. No one."

I was shaking, but I nodded. "I looked into changing my name once, but you don't understand how powerful these people are. There is nowhere I could hide that they couldn't find me if they wanted to. I made sure I did nothing that would make them want to."

He reached for me, then said, "If you want a hug, I need one as much as you do."

I searched his face. There was only love. How could that be? How could he have seen the ugliest of who I was and not want to run from it? "I may always panic when I'm cornered."

He wiped the tears from his cheek and said, "You think that makes you weak? You are one of the strongest people I've ever met. What they did to you was criminal, but you survived. They didn't break you, Caterina. They may have tried, but they didn't. I want to take a sledgehammer to everyone involved."

I smiled without humor. "I considered that in the beginning. I used to fantasize about going full-on sniper, but some days I feel like I'm holding on to my humanity by a thread. I can't let them take that last piece of me."

"If Cleaven Hills still exists, it won't for long. I'll make sure of that."

Fear rushed in. "Don't. Please. These people are dangerous."

He did hug me then. "I won't do anything foolish, but I need to make sure they're not doing to anyone else what they did to you."

I hugged him as tight as I could. "Don't go up against them, Benjamin. I can't lose you too."

"You won't. Don't even think that. You're safe, Caterina."

I felt safe and loved even though he hadn't said the words. Benjamin was the only person I'd told my whole story to. Finally vocalizing what had happened to me felt like the first swipe I'd taken at the junk car with the sledgehammer. It felt good, but I could do better.

I raised my hands to cup his face. "Thank you, Benjamin." The kiss I gave him was full of all the confusing emotions swirling within me. It was both too much and not enough at the same time. His lips were gentle even as mine were rough and frenzied. When I broke off the kiss I was a wreck inside and out. "What do you even see in me?"

He ran a thumb lightly over my parted lips. "Someone so damn beautiful she's inspiring me to be the man I should have been all along."

"I feel beautiful when you look at me that way."

His smile was tender. "That's because you are. And when you look at me the way you're doing, I easily imagine spending the rest of my life proving that to you."

I swallowed hard. "You don't have to say that."

"You don't have to believe it yet. It won't change how I feel."

"Where do we go from here?"

His smile was warm and reassuring. "When you get home tonight, I'll call you. Tomorrow morning we'll start the day the same way we did this past week. I'd love to visit your workplace. You're welcome to come visit mine. I know how I feel, Caterina. I'm all in. Are you?"

Holy shit. "Yes. Oh my God, yes."

If I'd discovered I was actually in a coma and that Benjamin wasn't real, I would have found a way to make it known that I didn't want to wake up. Let me be in this place just a little longer. Please don't wake me up.

Chapter Fifteen

Benjamin

I TOLD CATERINA that we would simply go back to normal after she opened up to me, but I couldn't. No man could have. I needed to do something about what I knew.

As I'd promised, I called Caterina that night to make sure she made it home from Salem. We talked about the fun we'd had that day and I encouraged her to call Emmie to tell her how great her cousin had been to us.

After we ended our call, I did an online search for anything related to Cleaven Hills. Nothing. I called several of my old friends and worked the name into the conversation. I had to know if anyone I knew had ever heard of it. They hadn't.

I didn't tell anyone why I was asking or even what the place was. I just needed to test if anyone would react to the name. None did. I broke down and even called my father. He asked me if it was a startup computer company.

Out of desperation I contacted someone I'd gone to college with who was known for doing some dubious hacking for international companies. I offered him a substantial, untraceable amount of crypto coin if he brought me any information about it. Late that night, he sent me a message saying if the place existed there was no trace of it online. Then he asked, "Are you sure this place even exists?"

I was. I didn't doubt a single thing Caterina had told me. Her pain was as real as her story.

A place that only the richest families in the world send their children to be "fixed." My family was wealthy, but we weren't at that level. I needed to find someone who was. There was no way I'd be able to rest until I'd found Cleaven Hills, tracked down anyone who had been part of it, and made them pay for what they had done to Caterina. I felt physically ill when I thought about the possibility that they might still be abusing others like her.

That's when it came to me that I did know someone who was so rich he would know about Cleaven Hills. Not only know about it, but have knowledge of how to contract their services because he already had—Clay Landon.

That fucking bastard. How could he have sentenced his sister to something like that? It was a question I knew needed to be asked in person, possibly while my hands were wrapped around his throat. I didn't waste my time contacting his office, instead I had my old hacking buddy locate his cell phone number and track it as well to get me his address. Thankfully that was something he was able to do.

Had I been thinking straight I would have brought a weapon with me when I drove to Clay's house. I would have also taken the time to come up with a plan for how to get him to talk. I wasn't thinking—I was acting—driven to do something because I couldn't stand back and do nothing.

It was late when I arrived at Clay's house. The butler told me he was already in bed for the night. I told his butler he'd have to wake him up because I had urgent family business to discuss with him.

It was urgent. I couldn't wait another minute to punch him in the face.

The butler took out his phone and sent a text. "He'll be right down. Please come in." He led the way to a sitting room.

A few minutes later Clay appeared in a robe and slippers with a small dog tucked beneath one of his arms. He handed the dog off to the butler and said, "Wake the nanny. Boppy will need to go out and then probably a snack. He doesn't go back to sleep when he's woken."

"Yes sir," the butler responded then hesitated as he looked back and forth between Clay and me.

"We're fine," Clay said, waving the butler off. "I know Benjamin, but if you see us here when you return, please bring two cups of coffee."

"This isn't a social visit," I growled once we were alone.

Clay took a seat, crossed one leg over another and adjusted his robe over both. "I know why you're here."

"I highly doubt that."

"You've been seeing Caterina. I have no problem with it. I looked into your family and they seem like a decent enough lot."

The fury that had been burning in my gut since Caterina had told me what happened to her welled up in me. "Don't pretend to care about your sister."

"I'm not pretending."

"I know everything."

"Then you know more than I do. I haven't understood Caterina's attitude for decades."

I closed the distance between us, towering over where he sat. "Stand up like a fucking man, look me in the eye, and tell me how you fucking live with yourself after what you did to her."

Slowly, Clay rose to his feet. "I don't know what Caterina told you, but our lack of a relationship is just as much her fault as mine. She's the one who wanted nothing to do with me. She's the one who wished me dead."

"No," I snarled, "all you did was send her away, ignore her, then pay animals to deal with her when you couldn't."

"I have no idea what you're talking about."

"Cleaven Hills."

"Is that supposed to mean something to me? It doesn't."

Not able to stomach his lies a moment more, I grabbed him by the neckline of his pajamas and hauled him up onto his toes. "I don't believe you, but I do believe you like your face the way it is, so if I were you I'd start talking before I start rearranging parts of your body."

Clay slapped at my hands. "Get your hands off me."

"Last chance. Warning, if I start beating you I don't know if I'll be able to stop. My only regret will be that you deserve so much more pain than I can deliver with my bare hands."

"Put him down," a female voice screamed. "What are

you doing?"

I didn't release Clay. "I'm giving this piece of shit a chance to do the right thing for once."

Clay looked me right in the eye. "Lexi, get out of here. Call the police."

"Call whoever you want, but you'll be dead before they get here if you don't tell me what I want to know. Cleaven Hills. I need to know everything you know about them."

Clay was pale and looked nervous, but he said, "I told you, I've never heard of them. How do they have anything to do with my sister?"

Rather than listening to her husband, Lexi picked up a vase and rushed toward us. She raised it above her head. "Let go of my husband."

"Lexi, no," Clay said, his voice suddenly sounding desperate. "Benjamin, I don't care what you do to me, but don't hurt Lexi. Lexi, please, go."

She stepped closer with the vase. "I'm not going anywhere, Clay. We're a team. I wish you'd let me hire that bodyguard I keep saying we should, but we can talk about that later. Right now I'm trying to remember the self-defense class I took in high school."

I gave Clay a good shake. "Don't make this worse than it needs to be. For God's sake, where is your humanity? Even if you don't care about Caterina, how can you look yourself in the mirror knowing that they might be out there, still hurting children because people like you pay them to?"

Lexi lowered the vase. "Clay, what is he talking about?"

"Yes, Clay," I growled. "Why don't you tell your sweet

wife what you did to Caterina? How you had her snatched from her boarding school and sent her off to be 'fixed' because you couldn't be bothered by her grief."

"I didn't send her anywhere." Clay gripped both of my wrists. "After my parents died, I went to England to help care for my grandparents. My grandfather was ill and he didn't trust anyone in the end. Caterina, Collin, and Cooper happily went off with my uncle. They wanted nothing to do with me. They blamed me for our parents' death. Since then, I've only had a handful of conversations with any of them and none of our exchanges were nice. They hate me."

I began to lower Clay to his feet. He was either a really good liar or he was telling the truth. "Of course they hated you. You chose money over them."

"No, I chose to take care of my grandparents while they went on with their lives. They were my siblings. Do you think I didn't care about them? I loved them. I called, but they never wanted to talk to me. I wrote, they never answered. They wanted nothing to do with me."

I released Clay. "That's not what Caterina told me."

"Well, then she lied," Clay said as Lexi rushed over to hug him.

No. "I don't believe that." I rubbed a hand over the back of my neck. "But I believe you believe she did." What the fuck was going on? "Where is your uncle now?"

Clay shook his head. "He went missing during a trip to Argentina. His body was never found."

"When? When did he go missing?"

"I don't know. I was twenty-four, I guess. He came to see

my grandmother after my grandfather died. They had a huge fight. I never saw him again after that."

I took a deep breath so I could go over the timeline in my head. "Caterina would have been in college by then."

"Yes, and had already turned her back on me, our grandmother, as well as legally signing off on her inheritance. She was very clear about wanting nothing to do with any of us."

"How could you not know what happened to her?" That was the hardest to swallow.

"What happened to her? She had to work her way through college? That was her decision."

"You don't fucking know, do you? How could you not? Caterina saw your signature." All I could do was shake my head.

"How would Caterina even know what my signature looks like?"

I hated that he was right. "Where's your grandmother now?"

"She died a few years after my grandfather did. She was never the same after losing him."

Or she was never the same after learning her own son was a monster and likely having him dealt with. I strode a few feet away. "No, I refuse to accept this." I advanced on him again. "With all the money you have, you have to know what Cleaven Hills is. Maybe you've heard about it by another name. It's where rich families send their children when they need them 'fixed.'"

Clay shook his head. "All we have is a dog. We call her

our baby and she does have her own nanny, but I won't even board her anywhere because I don't trust anyone to take care of her the way we do."

"I wish you'd cared that much about your family."

Lexi waved her hands in the air. "This is insane. Who are you?"

Clay straightened his robe and said, "Lexi, this is Benjamin Drover. I told you about him. He wanted to donate money to our Gold Star Initiative and I said no. I heard through the grapevine that he has been dating my sister. Until tonight I thought that was a good thing."

Eyes flashing like a protective mama bear, Lexi said, "I'm going to need you to start at the beginning, Benjamin, because I know Clay and he would never hurt anyone intentionally. So whatever you think you know about him is wrong."

I ran my hands through my hair. "Someone hired Cleaven Hills to deal with Caterina. They 'dealt' with her for over a year and if you don't know what that means, then you need to wise up. When she needed you the most, you failed her, Clay. And when you find out how badly, it's going to be a hard truth to live with."

Clay stepped away from his wife and came to stand before me. "Tell me."

Was he a sick bastard who wanted to revel in hearing about his handiwork or a sad pawn in someone else's game? "First tell me what your uncle and grandmother argued about."

"I don't know all of it. I heard the beginning of the conversation. He came to her for money because apparently he'd gone through all of his."

And if I had to guess, Caterina's as well as Collin's and Cooper's. "You heard nothing else?"

"My grandmother sent me out on an errand for her. When I came back he was gone. The house staff said it had been an ugly fight, but they didn't tell me what it was about. I assumed it was all money related."

Isn't it always? No wonder Caterina wants nothing to do with money. "Your uncle lied to you about your siblings. They wanted to be with you. Seems like he lied to all of you. I didn't understand at first why he would send Collin, Caterina, and Cooper to three different boarding schools, but I think I do now. He wanted to isolate and control them. He would have had access to the money your grandmother provided for their care. All he had to do to maintain control was keep a rift between all of you. He probably set you all up so that on the rare occasion when you did meet up you already didn't trust each other."

"Until my grandmother found out what he'd done."

"It seems that way."

"So, is Cleaven Hills a boarding school?"

"Oh, no," I said, "it's something much, much worse." When I'd set out to confront Clay I'd had no intention of telling him what had happened to Caterina, but in a monotone I told Clay everything Caterina had told me. I didn't leave out one fucking detail, not even when Lexi started to cry or when he looked about to throw up. He needed to know, because I needed his help to shut Cleaven Hills down for good.

When I finished I waited.

Clay wrapped his arms around his wife as she cried, but he met my gaze over her head. "I had no idea."

"I believe you, but now that you do, what are you doing about it?"

"I'm going to fucking destroy them. Every last one of them."

"So you do know who they are." For his sake I prayed he hadn't lied to me.

He shook his head. "No, I don't, but I have friends who are really good at digging up stuff like this." He took out his phone and made a call right then. "Bradford, I have a problem I need help with. Could you come to my house tomorrow morning? Yes, it's important and no you shouldn't tell anyone about this call. Except Ian. We need someone to make sure we don't all end up in jail. Yes. See you then." After he ended the call he said, "Consider Cleaven Hills handled."

"I'm going to need a little more than your word to do that."

"I'll bring you whatever proof you need, but you have to know that the people I called in are experts. They leave no footprints—and no survivors. The less you know about what goes down the better."

"All I care about is that they are shut down and if they're currently 'treating' anyone, those children end up somewhere safe."

"They will. I don't care what it costs me, they will."

Lexi raised her head. "I don't know what I would do if I knew anyone had hurt Willa. Clay, you have to go to Caterina. Tell her you love her."

He nodded. "I will."

I warned, "Tread softly with her, Clay. I wouldn't have told you any of this if I didn't need your help to stop it. She doesn't believe you care about her and it'll take time to win her trust."

"I'll find a way to show her that I never stopped caring about her."

"Don't let on that you know what happened to her. It might have been hard for you to hear about, but she lived it. It would only hurt her more if she thought people knew."

"I've already hurt her more than I ever meant to. I won't say anything."

Could I trust him?

I had no idea, but I'd gotten what I came for. "I'll need updates on Cleaven Hills. I don't care if it implicates me in something. I need to know."

"Understood."

Chapter Sixteen

Caterina

I'M HERE TO see Mr. Drover," I said a few days later when I went into the city to meet Benjamin for lunch at his office. The woman behind the desk rose to her feet with a huge smile on her face.

"You must be Caterina Landon."

"I am. You're welcome to call me Caterina."

The woman touched her chest. "My name is Harami. It's a real pleasure to meet you."

I found myself smiling back. She was so warm and welcoming it was impossible to feel out of place there. "Benjamin has told me a lot about you—all wonderful."

"Benjamin is a good man. I've heard some about you as well and I'm so happy he found you."

"I'm pretty happy about that as well," I said lightly.

"I'll tell him you're here." Harami picked up the phone receiver from her desk.

"No need," Benjamin announced as he walked into the office. He stopped right in front of me and greeted me with a quick, light kiss then took my hand. "I've missed you."

My cheeks warmed right along with my heart. "You saw me on Monday."

His grin was open and inviting. "But not yesterday."

When his hands went to my hips to pull me against him, I looked around and realized that Harami had stepped out of her office. "She's gone."

Benjamin looped his arms around my waist and bent to nuzzle my neck. "Smartest PA I've ever had."

With mock outrage, I said, "So you've trained her to give you time alone when a woman comes to your office?"

He raised his head and looked me in the eye. "The only woman I've ever brought here was Tasha and only once I knew we were serious."

My mouth dropped open and I swayed against him. Did that mean what I thought it meant? No. It couldn't. What did someone say to that? "Then I'm . . ." Excited. Scared shitless. Overwhelmed but in the best way. ". . . honored."

There was a twinkle in his eyes when he bent so his mouth was just above mine and growled, "You should be. Now how about kissing me like you missed me too."

I ran my hands up his chest, over his strong shoulders, then linked them behind his neck. Feeling his arousal grow in response gave me courage. From breasts to hips, I writhed my body against his. "Like this?" I went onto my tiptoes and claimed his mouth as mine.

Since our talk on the way back from driving monster trucks my inhibitions with Benjamin had begun to fall away. I'd shown him my deepest, darkest secrets and he'd stayed. Not only stayed, but seemed to care about me even more now that he knew me better. My anger and shame had less power over me when he looked down at me with—if that wasn't love I didn't know what love looked like.

Passion rocked through me and I forgot to hold back. I flicked my tongue between his lips, then deepened our kiss deliciously. He was all around me, dancing deep within my mouth, filling all of my senses and it was so damn wonderful I didn't care where we were.

When he raised his head, he was smiling. "I guess that'll do."

"Oh, really?" I joked, moving sensually against him. "And here I thought we had a connection."

"I'd love to connect with you," he wiggled his eyebrows playfully, "but not on my PA's desk."

"Gotcha. Location. Location. Location." Flirting with him had become as easy as breathing.

He chuckled. "She'd kick my ass."

"And since I like your ass the way it is, I guess we should behave ourselves."

"I do have a nice ass." He did a little butt wiggle that had me laughing against his chest.

"You're crazy," I said.

"Only for you," he answered and gave my forehead a kiss. "So are you ready for lunch? I thought we'd go somewhere we could walk to. Do you like Thai?"

"Love it."

"There's a little place about a block away. It might be busy but it's worth it."

"I'm in." We linked hands and strolled to the elevator

together. "So the ladies haven't stopped talking about you since we hung out with them. They keep asking when you'll be back, and they request that when you do return you wear that black T-shirt again because apparently it makes your arms drool worthy."

He laughed as we entered the elevator and tucked me to his side as we rode down together. "Your friends were a hoot. We should do something with them and their husbands. A huge quadruple date dinner. I need to know if they married men who are as funny as they are."

He was serious. "That would be amazing."

"Then set it up and let's make it happen."

How natural it felt to be with Benjamin still took me by surprise. When we'd parted in Salem after going up to New Hampshire, I'd been afraid I might not hear from him again. He'd called me that night, though, just as he said he would. And the next morning.

We didn't revisit what I'd shared with him and I was grateful for that. I didn't want to be defined by the worst time of my life. I'd faced that demon, even taken it out to show Benjamin, but it didn't belong in my day-to-day life. Without it I was free to simply enjoy being with a man who enjoyed being with me—a man I didn't have to lie to or hide my history from. I could finally have unguarded conversations without the worry that I might say something that didn't match the new life I'd chosen.

One day I hoped to be as real with Lorraine and the others. I didn't need to share my trauma with them, but I did yearn for them to know enough of my journey so that I didn't feel like I was pretending to be someone I wasn't. One day soon I'd be brave enough to let them in.

I stepped out of the elevator with Benjamin and smiled up at him. He was the reason I was feeling more comfortable with myself. I wondered if he had any idea how much his acceptance meant to me.

During our late-night phone call the night before he'd said something that was still echoing in my heart. He'd said I was helping him heal as well. Then he really opened up and told me about his marriage to Tasha, how he saw now that he'd failed her just as badly as he'd thought she'd failed him. When he explained how that realization had moved him to put her memorial case on his mantel to honor her memory, I fell the rest of the way in love with him. No, he wasn't perfect, nor was I. He was a good man with a heart of gold—a man who made mistakes but learned from them. He was open about his own struggles and because of that whatever shame I'd felt after sharing my ordeal with Cleaven Hills fell away.

I wasn't a big believer in fate—but maybe, just maybe, we really had been put in each other's paths to heal each other.

Just outside the office building, Benjamin looked down at me and asked, "What are you thinking?"

"That I lo—that I am so happy to be here today." How I'd felt had almost come out, but I wasn't ready to say it and worried that he might not be ready to hear it.

"I'm glad." He leaned in for a kiss then resumed walking. "My parents keep asking about you. They'd love to have us over to their house for dinner. I told them we need a little time before we're at that step, but when you're ready for that tell me."

When I'm ready? Did that mean he was? Was I? Things were going so fast. "Do you know what will make that easy? I won't even need to say the words. I can just hand you one of the boxes you sent me with those chocolates. I believe that was on one of them."

He groaned and chuckled. "I bet it was. You sent me off-balance from the first time we met. I don't do impulsive things like that and that was a reminder of why."

I hugged him as we walked. It was fun to tease him. "It's adorable now."

He laughed again and shook his head. "I suppose I'm lucky you didn't call the police."

"Oh, it wasn't that bad. Plus, I've already eaten some of the chocolates."

"Really? Care to share which ones?"

"I've had happy days since you sent them. And sad days."

He nodded.

I glanced at him out of the corner of my eye. "Almost right away I ate the one about not being able to stop thinking about you."

His grin was sexy as hell. "I wonder if those chocolates come with more intimate messages."

I laughed and blushed. "If not, we could always make our own."

"Now that is a craft I could get into."

Chapter Seventeen

Benjamin

LAUGHING WITH CATERINA in a booth at my favorite Thai restaurant was enough to convince me that I was handling the situation correctly. Things could have gotten awkward after what she'd shared with me. I could tell she was worried it would change how I felt about her.

It had.

I'd realized that there was nothing casual about how I felt about Caterina. She was the one for me. And, God willing, she'd realize I was the one for her.

Love.

I'd thought I knew what it meant, but I was only just beginning to. Caterina's happiness mattered to me as much, if not more, than my own. I wanted to treasure her, pamper her, help her make the life for herself that she'd always wanted.

It had taken seeing what she was hiding for me to know I was up to the task. She saw weakness in every way her trauma had changed her; I saw strength and resilience in those same characteristics. She was a brave survivor who had never given up on her family or on making a normal life for herself. Despite how her family had let her down, she'd kept her heart open to them and kept trying. Like Tasha, she was a fighter, a warrior, and this time my eyes were open to the beauty of that.

I understood her fears for her safety as well as for me. Until Cleaven Hills was tracked down and dealt with, I couldn't honestly tell her we were both safe. If they were well connected they might prove dangerous. Later, when I was convinced it was safe, I could support her reconciliation with Clay if that was what she wanted. I had no doubt that he would reach out to her again. By far, he wasn't one of my favorite people, but I did believe that he'd been lied to and manipulated by the same person Caterina had been. If her uncle wasn't already in hell, I'd make damn sure he visited that kind of torment on earth.

"Benjamin?" Caterina asked.

I shook my head to clear away my dark thoughts. "Sorry. What were you saying?"

Her smile was shy. "Do you have a busy afternoon?"

The look in her eyes was one every man lives for. I had to shift my position as a good portion of my blood headed down to my cock. "Nothing I couldn't reschedule."

She took a sip of water then met my gaze again. "I have the afternoon free."

I whipped out my phone and sent a text off to Harami. "Now, so do I."

There was a pulsing tension to the moment. "I'm craving a good dessert, but nothing from the menu here. Would you like to come back to my place for—chocolate?"

I wanted to shout, "Hell, yes," toss her over my shoulder, and haul her out of there, but I understood her well enough to know that her confidence came from her being able to set the pace. I cleared my throat. "I love chocolate. I'm in."

Her smile was sinfully adorable. She raised a hand and said, "Check, please."

Concern for her kept my enthusiasm in check. I remembered how quickly fun had turned to panic for her with the monster trucks. Sex with her might be fucking fantastic or it could be a heart-wrenching reminder for her of the abuse she'd endured. I couldn't erase her fears, but I could respect them and not let my own excitement blind me to what she wanted.

With sex I was used to taking the lead, but that was a role she might need to take—at least until we were more comfortable together. As I returned her smile I marveled at how okay I was with that.

We walked hand in hand to her car. I waited to be invited to ride with her and then slid into the passenger seat happily. My reward was the sexy smile she shot me as she pulled out into traffic. "Look at me, stealing you away from work in the middle of the day."

I loved the confidence in her and the way she was keeping her walls down with me. We were friends as well as soon-to-be lovers. I'd never had that with a woman. Because it was an issue we could remedy on our way to her place, I said, "I don't have any protection with me."

She bit her bottom lip then pulled into the parking lot of

a pharmacy. After hesitating, she chose the drive-through lane. At the window, she looked first at me, then raised her chin and requested a box of condoms.

The young male pharmacist nodded. I'm sure we weren't the first to ask him for some. I leaned over Caterina and added, "Large."

Looking like she was holding in a giggle, Caterina said, "And ribbed."

It might have been the pharmacist's poker face, but I couldn't help myself. I asked, "Do you have a pleasure pack?"

"Oh," Caterina said with a clap of her hands, "and anything flavored?"

I gurgled on laughter rising in me. "Some warming lotion?"

The pharmacist cocked an eyebrow. "You're welcome to come in and see what we have."

I could barely contain my mirth any longer. "That's okay, just fill a bag with whatever you think we might need."

As soon as the pharmacist walked away, Caterina and I started laughing like kids caught doing something naughty. "Did you see his face?" she asked.

"I hope he is at least laughing with us."

A few minutes later Caterina insisted on paying for the items when the man sent us a bag through the chute. I waited until we had pulled back out onto the street before I looked through the contents of the bag. There was more than one box of condoms—a rather impressive assortment. He'd included a flavored lubricant, a warming massage lotion and . . . I barked out a laugh. "He added a pregnancy test. What a little shit." I dug deeper and pulled out an invitation to a baby shower then a congratulatory card for an engagement. "We need to be that man's friend."

Caterina was wiping tears of laughter from her eyes. "Oh my God, we do."

We. It was amazing how easy it had become to think of future events in those terms. "Caterina. I—"

A car cut us off and she swerved to avoid it. We were both thrown to the side until she righted the car. "That was close."

"Yes, it was." I put my hand on her thigh and let out a long breath. I had been close. I'd been just about to blurt out that I loved her right then and there. Talk about rushing forward and possibly making her feel cornered. I needed to keep my head and go slowly.

The contents of the bag had partially spilled onto my lap. It was difficult to keep my cool while moving boxes of condoms off my already rock-hard cock.

Down boy, we're taking this slowly.

Chapter Eighteen

Caterina

A S I UNLOCKED the door to my apartment my hand shook with anticipation. I was a jumble of sexual tension and giddy joy. This wouldn't just be sex, it would be sex with a man who had gone from a temptation, to a friend, to a man I couldn't imagine my life without.

This was the natural next step and one I wasn't afraid to take. Those silly invitations the pharmacist had tossed into the bag had been meant as a joke, but they'd served as a reminder that those were the things I actually wanted. Until Benjamin I'd never met anyone with whom I'd considered either a possibility.

I could see myself making a life with Benjamin. He was strong and steady, kind and attentive. When I was with him I felt like I was capable of being all of that as well.

Benjamin followed me into my apartment and put the bag down on a table once we were inside. He turned to me and just stood there, hands in pockets, waiting.

I fell even more for him then. His excitement was visible and worthy of those large condoms, but he was making sure

I was comfortable. He'd heard me, and not only had he not judged me, he'd become even more caring because of it. His restraint allowed me the freedom to explore my own needs.

What did I want our first experience to be like?

A wave of gratitude washed over me as I realized he'd made that question possible. "Thank you for . . ." I didn't know how to express what I was feeling without risking letting the past charge in to overshadow the moment.

He smiled without approaching. "Whatever you're feeling, know that I'm just as grateful as you. I was in a dark place before you came into my life. I'm not saying I have all the answers now, but I'm finally at the point where I can face the questions. And when I do that, they lose their power over me."

"Yes." He'd said it so much better than I could have. "I like who I am lately and I haven't been able to say that in a long time."

"Me too."

Any other man would already be all over me, removing my clothing, rushing to free himself from his own. Allowing me to choose how to proceed was wonderful, but it also meant I needed to express what I wanted. The realization that I wasn't used to doing that both saddened me and opened my heart more to Benjamin. He'd not only said I deserved better, he was giving me room to discover how important it was that I play an active role in shaping my future.

I cleared my throat. "Are you up for a little game?"

"I'm up for whatever you want to do. Literally."

I'd never felt comfortable enough with a man to suggest a game and that saddened me. Why had I had sex with them then? To prove to myself that I was okay? I wished I could go back and tell myself not to fuck anyone who couldn't laugh with me as we ordered condoms at a pharmacy drive through. My thoughts must have shown on my face, because Benjamin's expression turned concerned.

"Caterina, we don't have to do anything. I'd be just as happy holding you while we watch a show. Or we can go out somewhere."

I took a step toward him. "I want you, Benjamin."

He started coughing and choking, then said, "You are making it really hard for me to keep my hands to myself." He took a step toward me. "I want you too."

I placed my hands on his chest. "That part wasn't the game."

His pulled me gently against him. "I sure as hell hope not."

I slid my hands upward to his strong neck. "I thought it might be fun to take turns saying what we'd like. I'll go first . . . I'd like you to kiss my neck." I tipped my head to one side.

He bent and kissed his way slowly up and down my neck. His breath was a hot tickle. His tongue teased its own trail behind my ear. Desire rocked through me.

Into my ear, he growled, "I'd like you to do whatever the hell you want."

I chuckled and met his gaze. "You'll have to be more specific if you want anything from me."

"Damn," he joked. "You're going to make me think about this." He didn't seem the least bit bothered by that. "I'd like you to rub your body back and forth against mine."

I did and he groaned with pleasure. "Yeah, just like that."

Feeling powerful and free, I said, "Kiss me."

"Gladly." His lips brushed over mine, gently at first then more firmly. As our kiss deepened, I moved my hands down and around to his back. My tongue met his eagerly. It was one hot, heavy, panty-wetting kiss that left me breathing heavily when he lifted his head.

He gave his stomach a pat and said, "Now climb on up here and you kiss me."

I didn't give myself time to question the logistics of it. I launched myself upward. He caught me easily and settled my legs around his waist. From there it was simply a matter of pulling his head downward so I could reach his lips. That kiss wiped the game right out of my head.

I started frantically unbuttoning his shirt. He lifted mine up and over my head. My bra hit the floor soon afterward. I arched my body so we were bare skin to bare skin, nipples to muscled chest. Between kisses, he walked with me still wrapped around his waist toward the table then said, "Grab that, will you? We're going to need it."

I did so then leaned back over his arm so my breasts were displayed for him. "Sure, as long as you do something for me as well."

"If I must," he joked before bringing a hand around to cup one of my breasts. When he brought his mouth down to it and began to tease its nipple with his teeth and tongue, I moaned and nearly dropped the bag. There was no rush to his moves. He thoroughly pleasured one then showed the same dedication to the other.

Never had I come so close to having an orgasm so early. With his hands beneath my ass, he adjusted my position and asked, "Bedroom?"

"Through there." I pointed to a door on the other side of my living room. Clutching our bag of protection in one hand I did my best to hold on to him as he walked. Once inside the bedroom, he lowered me to the floor, took the bag from me, placed it on the bedside table and stripped off the rest of his clothing.

His huge cock waved at full mast between us. "I'd like to taste you," he growled then lay down on the bed on his back. "You are formally invited to sit on my face."

I almost laughed but decided a better response was to quickly strip off my remaining clothing and climb onto the bed with him. I'd received oral sex before, but never like this. I'd never felt so in control. Facing the headboard of my bed, I straddled his face and positioned my sex just above his mouth.

One of his hands cupped my now bare ass. His other hand came up between my legs and parted my sex to give him better access. From then on it was pure ecstasy. His tongue worshiped, teased, plunged. His teeth grazed, nibbled, tugged gently. He was relentlessly, tirelessly talented and bold. I clung to my headboard as he brought me to the edge of release and then sent me over the edge.

Shaken, and even more hungry for him, I moved downward until I was straddling his hips and the tip of his cock brushed against my wet sex. "That was amazing."

He wiped a hand across his mouth then grinned. "Aw, shucks, you ain't seen nothing yet."

I leaned over to the bag and pulled out a box of condoms. I meant for it to be a sophisticated move but when I ripped the top off too hard condoms came flying out, landing all over the bed and his chest.

He chuckled. "I like your enthusiasm."

"Hush," I joked. "This is supposed to be sexy."

With a thrust of his hips he dipped the tip of his cock between the lips of my sex and almost inside me. "If you need more proof that everything you're doing is working for me I'll give it to—as deep and as hard as you want."

I shuddered with pleasure and opened a foil package. "Deep and hard is how I like it."

He took the condom from me and slid it on. "I knew we had a lot in common." His hands settled on my hips. "Top or bottom?"

"Both?"

"Deal." He lifted me above his cock and lowered me onto it, slowly filling me, stretching me to accommodate his large size. Once he was fully in he began to move in and out so slowly I became impatient and ground myself down onto him, meeting him thrust for thrust, increasing our speed as I did.

I bent and kissed him, brushing my excited nipples over his chest. He pounded up into me. Deeper and wilder. Faster and faster. I rode him until I was close to coming for the second time.

Then he rolled me beneath him and put my legs up around his neck. When he thrust inside me, he hit a spot that brought my pleasure to a whole new level. I cried out his name. He powerfully thrust into me again and again. I was out of my mind as wave after wave of heat spiraled through me. He felt so fucking good in me. He moved one of my legs out to one side and drove himself even deeper. And I glimpsed heaven.

Thrust after thrust, hard and fast, he pounded down into me. I was digging my nails into his shoulders and begging him not to stop. He didn't. I came with a glorious release and he joined me with a guttural sound and one final thrust.

We collapsed beside each other. He turned briefly to clean himself off then took me into his arms. The kiss he gave me was so tender and sweet I almost burst into tears.

Running a hand through my hair, he said, "I love you, Caterina. If it's too early for you to hear it, I'll hold off and say it again only when you're okay with it—but you need to know how I feel."

My eyes misted and I fought back those damn tears again. "I love you too, Benjamin."

"You can call me Ben," he said lightly.

The bit of comic relief was needed. I sniffed and said, "And you can call me . . . Caterina." I laid my head on his chest and tried to wrap my mind around what had just happened. "You love me?"

His chest rumbled with a chuckle. "I thought we'd clarified that."

"This is real."

He lifted his head and looked at me. "More real than anything has ever been for me."

The love in his eyes had my eyes welling up again. "I will not cry. I refuse to."

He cupped one of my breasts and dipped his head down to kiss its nipple before saying, "You're a crier, but it's cute."

"Cute?" I tried to summon outrage, but none came. "No woman likes to be called cute."

He ran a hand down my stomach to my sex. One of his fingers slid between my folds and began to gently circle my clit. "You don't like it? Not even a little bit?"

I spread my legs for him, my breath becoming shallow as his touch lit a fire in me again. "I guess I don't mind it."

He dipped a finger inside me. "I wouldn't want to do anything you don't like."

I closed my eyes and jutted against his hand. "No worry about that."

In my ear he whispered, "There's nothing about you I don't love, Caterina. Laughing, crying, coming in my mouth—I want it all." He thrust a second finger inside me and began to pump them in and out while his thumb moved back and forth over my clit. "You're beautiful, Caterina. So damn beautiful on the inside and outside. I want to spend the rest of my life showing you how much you mean to me."

I wanted to hear what he was saying, but it was impossible to concentrate on his sweet words while his hand was working its magic. I encircled his already hardening cock with my hand and pleaded, "Maybe we don't need to talk as much."

"Yes, ma'am." His laugh was as sexy as what he was doing physically.

A partner, a lover, and more importantly a friend. A really good friend who knew how to do the most amazing things with those fingers of his.

We spent the afternoon and most of the night working our way through the contents of the bag we'd gotten at the pharmacy.

Chapter Nineteen

Benjamin

I HELD CATERINA long after she fell asleep. I'd never talked as much during sex, but I'd never laughed as much either. Being with her had been fucking fantastic, but that hadn't been surprising. All she had to do was look at me and I burned for her. My heart ached at the thought that anyone had ever hurt this woman . . . and an anger churned my gut at the possibility that they were still out there hurting others.

I'd told Clay the details of the trauma his sister had suffered because without that information he would not have understood the severity of how his family had failed her. I wasn't a superhero in a movie nor did I apparently have connections to the type of people who would have any knowledge of Cleaven Hills. Thank God. I couldn't imagine what my reaction would have been had I discovered people in my circle had utilized their services . . . or even knew anyone who would.

Unfortunately, that meant I was relying on Clay to step up for the sake of a sister he had until recently denied the existence of. Had telling him been a mistake? If so, it wasn't one I could undo.

Caterina shifted against me, snuggled closer. I kissed her forehead before lying back and closing my eyes. What she'd been through wasn't something someone "got over." I thought back over all the hints she'd dropped along the way about how it still affected her and they all made sense. They also made her trust in me that much more meaningful.

I didn't know what I expected her to say in response to my announcement that I loved her. I wasn't a man who said those words easily. I'd said them at fifteen to the seventeen-year-old girl who initiated me to the pleasure of giving and receiving oral sex. A young man sometimes confuses gratitude for something like that with deeper feelings.

I'd said them to Tasha and at the time had thought I understood what love was. I hadn't. I'd still been too concerned with myself and what I wanted.

So many of the songs I'd thought were ridiculous and cornball began to hit home when I heard them now. I finally understood that love was about so much more than sexual compatibility. I'd wanted Caterina, had spent a good portion of the day fantasizing about what we'd just done, but if she'd have said she wanted to wait . . . I would have waited. A day. A month. A year. It wouldn't have mattered.

If she woke up and said she wanted to be with me, but sex would need to be tabled for a while . . . I'd be okay with that. I might tire out one or both of my hands, but I wouldn't look elsewhere for relief. Other women, and there had been a good number of them, held no appeal to me anymore. I'd found my other half.

And she loves me.

I fell asleep with my arms around Caterina and a smile on my face.

Late the next morning, I woke to my phone buzzing from an incoming text. I carefully slid my arm out from under Caterina, stepped into my boxers, and hunted down my phone.

Call me—Clay.

Shit. I left the bedroom and closed the door behind me. Even though I was in no mood to talk to him, there was a chance it might be something important. "What do you need, Clay?" I asked in a voice low enough it shouldn't carry through the apartment.

"Are you on a secure line?"

"I'm on my cell phone."

"Don't say anything unless it is in code."

I rubbed a hand over my face. He was so dramatic. "Sure. What's up?"

"The car issue we discussed the other day has been addressed. I took it to the best mechanics I know. They hunted down the issue. It wasn't easy. They had to tear your car apart. Piece by piece. Some of the parts didn't survive, but they won't be replaced. Consider the car totaled. It will never drive again."

I sat down on the couch. "Were there any passengers?"

"A few. It was as you described. Some were in rough condition. If it was possible, they were released from care to parents who understand now to never let anyone else drive their children around. We have one passenger who doesn't trust her parents to drive her anywhere so we're working on finding a good option for her."

"If she needs anything—"

"We have it covered." After a pause, he said, "Tell no one about this. Sadly, the makers of this vehicle were well connected. Really well connected. They had some good reviews and loyal supporters, but none held up under scrutiny. It took some . . . persuading to get the manufacturer's information. We did, though, because it doesn't really matter if we scrapped one of their cars if they continue to put them on the road."

"How can you be sure that won't happen?"

"You don't know the mechanics I called in. They're— meticulous. And now that this brand of vehicle is on their radar they'll be watching for it."

If what he was saying was true I was right to tell him about Caterina. "Thank you for dealing with this issue. I was having trouble sleeping knowing that someone else might be riding around in a similar vehicle."

"Speaking of passengers, I want to see Caterina. I have to tell her I didn't know."

"You might not want to start there. What she wants more than anything else is to know that you care. Once she believes that, she might believe the rest."

"I thought she wanted nothing to do with me. I reached out to her but was always told she didn't want to talk to me. And every time I saw her, what she said supported that." He cleared his throat then said, "I didn't endure what she did, but I suffered as well."

"I wouldn't start with that either. Listen, you were both manipulated. From what I can tell you were deliberately separated, isolated, and then your siblings were milked of their money. Your uncle couldn't get to you because you were with your grandparents. Put how you feel aside and ask yourself what it was like to be any of your siblings. One killed himself, one is still struggling with what she went through, and I don't know how Cooper faired but my guess is not much better if he is MIA."

"Collin didn't kill himself. He overdosed at a party. He was heavy into drinking and drugs."

"Because?"

"No. You're not laying this at my door. I tried. My grandmother needed help caring for my grandfather. They needed me too. Even when my grandfather became violent from dementia I cared for him so no one would know. I am not a bad person."

"I have no idea if you are or aren't." Shaking my head, I felt a good amount of pity for Caterina's family. She and her siblings had lost their parents. Their grandmother had apparently been distracted by her husband's illness. The eldest, Clay, had been called on to help, leaving Collin, Caterina, and Cooper vulnerable for someone like their uncle to take advantage and he had. There had to be a special place in hell for someone like that. "I don't care why you weren't there for Caterina a decade ago. What matters to me is what you do now. Do you care about her at all?"

"Of course I do."

"There is no 'of course' in any of this. You haven't

shown her that you do. She needs to see it. If you can put your pride and your excuses aside you could have a real relationship with your sister. Think about it."

"I'd call her, but I don't know what to say."

Nor did I when it came to navigating that conversation. I was flying by the seat of my pants, hoping I said something that would help. If Caterina's happiness wasn't tied up with working things out with Clay, I would have had no patience with him. For her, I tried to understand him enough to guide him. "Tell her you're sorry. Tell her you love her."

"She won't believe me. I've tried."

"Then you haven't done it the right way. Try harder."

"Try harder." He repeated my words. "You're right. In the past I've given up too easily. I know what I need to do now."

"Don't tell her that I said anything. Let her tell you in her own time. Go slow. She needs—" I ended the call when I heard footsteps approaching.

"Benjamin?" Caterina asked from the doorway of her bedroom. Her hair was wild from sleep and she was wearing my shirt. "Everything okay?"

I tossed my phone down on the table beside the couch and nodded. "I believe so." I sighed, closed the distance between us, wrapped my arms around her, and buried my face in her neck. Had she heard any of the phone call? I hoped not. "Did I wake you?"

Her arms slid up and around my neck. "You did, but I'm willing to forgive you for that."

I smiled. "How kind of you."

She moved seductively back and forth against me. "For some reason, I'm feeling mellow and at one with the universe today."

With one strong move, I swept her up into my arms. "I can't imagine what that reason might be."

She laughed and laid her head on my shoulder as I carried her back to the bedroom. "It might have been that third orgasm. Or possibly the fourth."

I stopped when I reached the bed and lowered her to her feet. "You know what they say about orgasms . . ."

"I don't, actually."

"An orgasm a day—" I was about to say something witty, but she slipped her hand beneath the waistband of my boxers and began to stroke my cock and my brain emptied.

"What?"

"Huh?"

"What does an orgasm a day do?"

"I have no idea, but I suggest we find out." With that, I kissed her and although we didn't talk nearly as much that time, it was just as good.

Chapter Twenty

Caterina

NEAR THE END of the following week, I was at a restaurant having lunch with my friends. Although they were as fun as usual, I was distracted. Things were going so well with Benjamin that I dismissed my worries as me getting scared and trying to sabotage it.

Keiona leaned over and touched my arm. "Earth to Caterina. Are you with us?"

I shook my head to clear it and forced a smile. "Sorry."

"Let her be," Emmie said. "New love is as exhausting as a new baby." She winked at me. "Both let you get very little sleep."

I blushed. It was true. Benjamin and I had spent every night together since we had sex, and although it was amazing, I was definitely not getting my normal eight hours of sleep.

Lorraine sighed. "I'd go back in a heartbeat to both . . . for a day . . . I do love a good nap."

"Oh, Lord," Keiona said. "We're not in our eighties. Maybe you should go rent another costume."

"Bitch," Lorraine said with a laugh.

Emmie covered a smile with her hand and said to me, "That struck a nerve."

"All I'm saying," Keiona said with a shrug, "is that you get out of your sex life what you put into it."

Lorraine sat back. "It's not always that easy." She swirled her coffee in her mug. "Sometimes it's not as enjoyable as it used to be."

Keiona's expression turned sympathetic. "That's normal. Have you spoken to your doctor?"

"I did. He said we just need more foreplay."

"Find another doctor," Keiona said. "One who understands the female body. A man has trouble with an orgasm and the medical field cures it ahead of cancer. A woman has the same issue and they tell us we're doing something wrong." She took out a piece of paper and wrote down a name and number. "This is the name of my doctor. A year ago I had a similar issue. Things got painful. She worked with me to figure out what I needed. And her first suggestion didn't work. But I'm fine now and glad that I addressed it."

Lorraine kept her eyes glued to her coffee mug. "It's embarrassing."

"It shouldn't be," Emmie said, "not with us."

"And not with your doctor," Keiona added.

Lorraine raised her eyes to each of ours in turn. When she got to me, her smile was sad. "Bet you're regretting hanging out with the older ladies now."

My throat was tight with emotion. "No, I feel very lucky to have found you all."

Keiona put her arm around Lorraine's shoulders. "I'm sorry I said what I did about the costume. I wouldn't have if I had known."

Lorraine hugged her back. "I know. It's not a problem."

"Not that this isn't important," Emmie said, "but can we go back to hearing about Caterina's new beau?"

All eyes flew to me. I grinned awkwardly. "He's great."

"But?" Keiona asked. "I hear a but."

"There's no—" I stopped, not wanting to lie to them. "I told him something very private and I think he might have told someone else."

"Oh," Lorraine said. "That's not good."

"Why do you think that?" Emmie asked.

"I overheard him on the phone. He was telling someone not to tell someone else that he'd said anything."

"That's pretty vague." Emmie weighed the air with her hands.

"Are you sure he was referring to you?" Keiona asked.

"No."

Lorraine wrinkled her nose. "Did you ask him about it?"

"No."

"So, you're just holding on to what you think he is guilty of without giving him a chance to explain himself?" Keiona arched an eyebrow.

"Yep." I slumped back in my seat. "That's pretty much what I'm doing."

"At least she's honest about it," Lorraine said in a light tone.

Emmie nodded. "We've all done that, but eventually you

figure out it's a whole lot easier if you just ask your man if he fucked up and let him apologize."

"Assuming he's actually guilty," Lorraine reminded.

"Oh, he did it," Emmie countered.

Keiona added, "One hundred percent. He probably thought he was helping. If you told him that something was bothering you he definitely did something to try to make it better. Men can't sit back and do nothing when the women they love are hurting."

My hand flew to my mouth as all kinds of possibilities flew through my mind. "I told him not to get involved."

Lorraine rolled her eyes. "That has only ever stopped a man—oh, never. They can't help themselves."

"And they say we're bad," Keiona said.

Emmie chuckled. "We kind of are. I know I can't stop myself sometimes. I just love him so much. If someone comes for my hubby I take it as a personal attack and they'd better watch their back. No one messes with my family."

"Ditto," Keiona said.

Lorraine touched my hand. "So, just ask him. Let him tell you his side. And if he screwed up, give him a chance to make it up to you because that man adores you."

"I'm pretty into him as well," I admitted.

"We know," Emmie joked. "You could work his name into a conversation about trash day pickup."

I laughed at that. "I'm not that bad." When none of the ladies agreed, I added, "Okay, but in my defense, I've never been in love before."

"Aww," Emmie said. "You love him."

"I do." My earlier worries began to fall away. "He's the first man who has ever taken the time to know me. Really know me. I thought no one would if I really let them in, but nothing I said scared him off. He said he loves me too."

"All a person has to do is see how he looks at you to see how true that is," Lorraine said.

I let myself bask in the good for once. "We've been inseparable this week. I'm either at his place or he's at mine. And it has been so wonderful. As soon as I'm ready for it, he said his parents want to meet me."

"Sounds like he's all in," Keiona said.

"He said he is. He also suggested we all go out sometime, all of you with your husbands."

Emmie got all dreamy. "I like him. Don't let this one get away."

"I'll try not to." Was it even in my control?

My phone lit with a message. I froze when I saw it was from Clay. *I handled seeing you badly. Please give me another chance.* That was followed by a request to see me and an address where he was. He said he'd be there for an hour. My hand shook and I put the phone down.

"Something wrong?" Lorraine asked with concern.

"I don't know." I picked up the phone and read the message again. "It's from my brother. He wants me to meet him right now."

Keiona said, "You didn't mention you have a brother."

"We're not close."

"But he wants to see you today?" Emmie asked.

"Right now."

"Ask him what he wants," Lorraine suggested.

I typed that question to Clay and waited. *I'll tell you when you get here.*

I shook my head and pushed my phone away. "No."

"What did he say?" Keiona asked.

"He said he'll tell me when I get there. I'm not going." I hugged my arms around myself. "No. I can't do it. I'm not doing that."

Lorraine and the others exchanged a look and the table fell silent while I fought back a mini panic attack. Clay and I had already said everything we needed to. I didn't want to hear his lies again.

A horrific thought came to me and once it took hold I began to shake. What if—what if Benjamin had accused Clay of sending me to Cleaven Hills? What if Clay intended to lure me out and silence me? I couldn't be taken as an adult, could I? I started to gasp for air at the idea that I could.

"It's okay," Emmie said. "We're here with you. Breathe."

My eyes blurred with tears. "I'm sorry." I waved a hand frantically.

Keiona took my hand in hers. "Look at me, Caterina. You're with friends. If someone is hurting you, you need to tell someone and we'll get you help."

The floodgates in my mind opened and ugly memories poured in, more than I could handle. All I could say was that I was sorry over and over. I bent over, feeling like I might get sick right there.

"Let's get her out in the air," Lorraine said. She paid the

bill and they ushered me out of the restaurant.

The sunshine and fresh air did help a little. I took several deep breaths. I can change my number. I can run away. I have enough money to go far, far away.

Keiona stood in front of me. "Caterina, is someone hurting you?"

I shook my head and admitted, "Not anymore, but I'm afraid they could again."

Emmie gasped.

With a hand on either of my shoulders, Keiona looked me in the eye. "They couldn't. I won't let them. Lorraine has family in law enforcement, we can call them. Hell, even Emmie will kick someone's ass for you. And you have Benjamin. None of us would ever let anything happen to you."

"You're safe," Lorraine said. "If you need it, I have a guest room at my house."

"Me too," Emmie said.

Keiona added, "Whatever it is, we probably know someone who can help. You're not alone."

I took another deep breath, then another. I'm not alone. "Thank you."

"Did your brother hurt you?" Emmie asked.

I shook my head. "It's complicated."

"Do you want to see him?" Lorraine looked from Emmie and Keiona back to me. "If so, we could go with you."

It took me a moment to absorb that. "You would do that?"

Emmie gave her purse a pat. "FYI, I'm always packing.

You can never be too safe."

Good to know. I did want to know what Clay wanted to tell me and now that my panic had subsided, I told myself I wouldn't go as easily this time if someone tried to take me. It made me regret that I'd told Benjamin to not look into Cleaven Hills. I'd been wrong. All I'd been thinking about was our safety, but on the heels of facing that they might come for me was the realization that someone else was already suffering at their hands.

While I do nothing.

I need to do something.

And the first step would involve Clay either way. Regardless of what he wanted to say to me, he'd know if they were still in existence and if they were how to track them down.

It was time to stop running.

"Okay." I pressed my lips together and nodded. "Let's go see what my brother wants."

I gave them the address. Emmie looked it up. "It's not too far. We could drive over there now."

Lorraine put an arm around me. "Call Benjamin."

With shaking hands I sent him a text: **Going to meet Clay. My friends are coming with me.** I included the address Clay provided.

Where are you? I'll meet you.

I wiped a stray tear from the corner of my eye and typed in the name of the restaurant.

I'll be right there. Give me ten.

Okay.

I hugged my phone to my chest. "Benjamin wants to meet us here and go with us."

Keiona nodded in approval. "I knew there was a reason I

liked him."

I took another calming breath. "I'm probably worried about nothing. My brother might just want to say something ridiculous to me."

"Doesn't matter. Friends don't let friends face crazy alone," Emmie said.

I half-laughed half-cried at that. "I love you guys."

Lorraine gave my arm a squeeze. "We love you right back. Now, where is the bathroom? Since we have time, I should pee before we go."

"Seriously?" Keiona asked with an eye roll.

"Like you don't have to also?" Lorraine challenged.

In a grudging tone, Keiona said, "Well now I do but just because you brought it up, not because I have an old bladder."

Emmie stayed with me while the two of them wandered away. "I have to pee too, but I'll wait until they come back. If they say anything rude to each other I'll laugh and likely piss myself. Then we'll have to stop at my house for fresh pants and there's no time for that."

It could have been because my emotions were all over the place, but I thought that was the fucking funniest thing anyone had ever said. I laughed so hard I almost nearly wet my pants.

Slightly amused, but also not, Emmie said, "Yeah, it's hilarious until something the size of a bowling ball comes out your vagina and you understand why there is a diaper aisle for adults."

I tried to stop laughing and started choking. "Stop. Please stop. I'm already scared enough."

Chapter Twenty-One

Benjamin

I CALLED CLAY on my way to Caterina, but he didn't answer. On one hand I was glad that he had taken my advice and reached out to her. On the other hand I hadn't told him how feeling cornered wasn't something Caterina handled well. I wanted to tell him to go easy.

Yes, I'd told him to go slow and easy—but this was Clay. He was damaged in his own way, probably on some diagnostic spectrum I wasn't qualified to determine. All I cared about was how his issues might affect Caterina.

I kicked myself mentally for not asking more questions. Had the meeting been his idea or hers? Why was she taking her friends with her? Was she happy about the meeting? When her text had come in I hadn't thought to ask for details. My gut had told me I needed to be with her when she faced him again.

So I was rushing to her, cursing every car going the speed limit. My heart was racing and my hands were sweaty as adrenaline pumped through me. My brain tried to tell my body that there was no danger. Caterina probably wasn't even upset. I could be reacting to a problem that didn't exist.

That wasn't what my gut said, though.

Something in me was certain she was in distress. How could I possibly get that from a text? I couldn't explain it. All I knew was I wouldn't breathe right until I saw for myself that she was okay.

As soon as I pulled into the parking lot, I saw Caterina and her friends standing outside. I drove up to where they were and jumped out, telling myself to calm down even as I sprinted around the car to her. She flew across the distance and into my arms. I hugged her to my chest, burying my face in her hair.

When she looked up at me, her eyes were dark and worried. "Clay asked to meet me today. He said he handled seeing me badly and would like a second chance. He has something to tell me, but he wouldn't say what."

Fucking Clay and his dramatics. He could have just apologized over the phone like a regular person. "He probably just wants to say he's sorry."

She searched my face. "You didn't talk to him again, did you? Tell me you didn't tell him what I told you."

"I did." I hated how she tensed in my arms and began to shake. "He needed to know and I needed his help to shut them down."

"No."

"Yes. They've been dealt with, Caterina. Not only are you safe, but now so are others who they had just like they had you. Clay has some powerful friends and they took care of it."

She backed out of my arms. Never before had I seen real terror in the eyes of someone I loved and I prayed I never would again. Just above a whisper, she asked, "Did he show you proof or did you just take his word for that? How do you know that this isn't a trick to get us somewhere where I could be taken again?"

I didn't know, not with a certainty that would stand up in the face of her fear. "I heard the call he made . . ." I ran a hand through my hair. "I don't know. You don't have to meet him."

Hugging her arms around herself, she said, "I do. I won't sleep if I don't. I'll spend the rest of my life looking over my shoulder wondering when someone is going to jump out of a car to take me. I need to know if what you said to him made him angry enough to do that to me again." Tears welled in her eyes. "You shouldn't have said anything to him."

"I couldn't do nothing. They were still hurting people."

"So you sacrificed me. And you don't know that they were even stopped. You don't know anything."

"I know that I love you and I would die to protect you." I reached out a hand to her, but she didn't take it. I let my hand fall. "You're right. I shouldn't have gone to him without discussing it with you. I was angry. I couldn't do nothing."

She was visibly shaking. "You think it was easy for me to keep quiet? I hate myself for hiding, for doing nothing to stop them from hurting someone else. They're too big to stop—too powerful. Now that they know I've told someone they won't let me live." Tears began to pour down her cheeks.

I glanced behind her to her friends who were huddled, worried but waiting. "Caterina, I won't let anything happen to you. When they took you, you were vulnerable and alone. You're not alone now. You have me. You have your friends. We will protect you." She nodded once, but I wasn't sure she heard me. "There's something you need to know." Carefully, with as little emotion as I could, I began to tell her what Clay had told me. I told her about how he'd been tasked to care for their grandfather, how he'd been told that none of his siblings wanted to see him, and about the fight her uncle had had with her grandmother before he disappeared. "I think your grandmother saw what he was doing, maybe not all of it, but she understood that he'd tried to manipulate all of you so he could get your money. I don't believe he ran away; I believe she took out her own son—for her grandchildren. The more I think about it, the more I wonder if he wasn't involved in the death of your parents."

Eyes wide, Caterina stood motionless, absorbing all I'd shared. She began to rub her upper arms as if she were fighting off cold. "If my uncle convinced Clay we hated him, was that why Clay had me sent away?"

"I don't believe Clay was responsible for that."

"I saw his signature."

"You saw a signature." I sighed. What if I was wrong? What if Clay was such a good liar that he'd fooled me? "Listen, this is like a horrible onion that when the layers are peeled away it reveals only more horror. I don't know what would make anyone do what your uncle did. I don't know if your brother is as innocent as he claims or if he was part of it, but I know that together we can face this. Together we can demand the proof. Don't you dare hate yourself for hiding. If you hadn't, you wouldn't be here to fight today. You couldn't fight this battle alone—no one could." I nodded toward her friends. "Do they know?"

"Not the details." She sniffed. "I can't live with the details. My mind has to shut them out or I would never leave the house. That might sound crazy—"

"No, that sounds normal." I'd done some reading about victims of trauma. What she was referencing was what made it often difficult for rape victims to be believed. The mind could block out what was too painful for it to remember. How could a woman not remember if they'd been penetrated or not? People who dealt with victims understood is was not only possible to forget something like that, it was likely someone would. Remembering was its own torture and not the simple face-it-to-heal-it journey many believed. When things calmed, I would encourage Caterina to talk to a professional . . . if she wanted to. And I could imagine the two of us funding a shelter for abused women or actively helping in another way. All of that, though, would come in time. One step at a time. "What do you want to do? Tell me how I can best support you right now."

She let out a breath as if she'd been holding it for a while. "You're already doing it. You're here." Her face crumpled. "I'm sorry about what I said earlier. I know you were trying to help."

"You have nothing to be sorry about. You said how you

felt." This time when I offered my hand to her, she took it. "Always do that. Always let me in. I'm not perfect, but I love you so much it hurts."

She stepped forward and hugged her arms around me again. "I love you the same way." We kissed then. It was full of passion and promise. When we broke it off there was a different look in her eyes. "I don't know what to believe about Clay, but I think I could hear him out now without running. I've spent a lot of time hating him as well as myself. If it wasn't his fault . . . if it was all my uncle . . . and he's gone . . . and if Clay really did take down Cleaven Hills . . ."

"You'd finally be safe."

She nodded and her arms tightened around me. "I want this to be true. I want it to be true so badly."

"So do I." Never had I said anything I meant more.

Chapter Twenty-Two

Caterina

A S WE DROVE to the address Clay had sent me, I glanced into the rearview mirror of Emmie's minivan and fell even more in love with Benjamin. He could have insisted I rode over with him in his high-priced car, but instead he was sandwiched between two of my friends Lorraine and Keiona, talking to them as if they were long-time friends.

And my friends? They'd waited patiently while I talked to Benjamin and graciously hadn't expected to be told what we discussed. They were there for support.

I tensed when we pulled onto the street where several black SUVs lined both sides of the street. I turned in my seat to check Benjamin's reaction and relaxed when I saw his reassuring smile. "I had my security team sent over for a little backup, just in case."

"Holy shit," Keiona said, "in case of what? What are we walking into?"

"Hopefully nothing," I said. "This is where I should probably tell you that I was born into a wealthy family. Very wealthy. I walked away from that, though. My brother didn't. And we've had issues. I don't know what today will be like."

Emmie parallel parked between two of the SUVs. "They say money doesn't make you happy and I guess they're right."

Lorraine said Emmie's name in reprimand. "Emmie, this isn't a joke."

"Oh, I get that," Emmie said. "Humor is my survival mechanism. Leave me in the car if you can't handle it."

I leaned over and touched her arm. "You make as many jokes as you need to, Emmie. I need them as much as you do."

She smiled and turned off the van engine. "So if I request that some of those hot, young, security guys watch me really carefully . . . like close enough for me to be able to smell them . . . that won't offend anyone, right?"

"You'd never know she's married," Keiona said lightly.

"Oh, I don't touch," Emmie said. "I don't even flirt. But looking? Why did God give us eyes if he didn't want us to see the beauty of his creations?"

Even Benjamin laughed at that.

We piled out of the van. Benjamin stepped aside to speak briefly with one of the men. It felt surreal and yet reassuring. Benjamin hadn't just joined the battle; he'd come equipped to win.

As we walked up the driveway of a large private home, only Emmie was flanked by security, which put enough humor in the situation that a good amount of my fear drained away. I linked my hand with his and said, "You're quite the ballbuster, aren't you?"

"Always," he said lightly. "But in a good way." He glanced back at Emmie. "Come on, you know I just made her day."

"You did." I smiled even though my emotions were all over the place. "Thank you."

"No, thank you. You might not believe this yet, but I need you just as much as you think you need me. I was sinking, Caterina. The first day we met you joked that we sounded perfect for each other, and you were right. Without you I would have gone the rest of my life not understanding what being a real partner to someone meant."

I wasn't given time to respond to that because the front door of the home opened to reveal Clay and a woman. He looked at us then at our entourage. "You brought friends," he said.

I came to a stop at the bottom of the steps. "I did and they all come inside or I don't."

His expression tightened and for a moment I thought he might burst into tears. "I understand. Bring who you need to." He put his arm around the woman next to him. "This is my wife, Lexi."

With Benjamin at my side I walked up the steps to meet them. She looked emotional but not scared or threatening. "It's nice to meet you, Lexi."

She held out a hand for me to shake. "I'm so glad you agreed to come."

I shook her hand because I wanted this to work out. I always had. "I hope I'll leave glad I came."

"You will," Clay said with confidence. "I've done a lot of thinking about how to fix things between us. You think I don't love you, that I never cared. I have always cared about you. I thought you didn't care about me. That's why I invited you here today. I want you to meet the family I made for myself when I felt like I didn't have one. They're going to love you."

I tensed. "You think I want to meet a family you created while your real family suffered without you?"

Clay looked to Lexi as if for help, then said, "I'm doing this wrong."

Lexi looked nearly as lost. "They're good people. Really good people."

"I don't care about them. I'm here for the truth." I raised my chin. "Clay, Benjamin said you had nothing to do with what happened to me. Look me in the eye and tell me if that's the truth."

He stepped forward, looking tormented. "I had no idea. I thought you were safe with our uncle. When I didn't hear from you, I didn't check on you because I thought you wanted nothing to do with me. I will regret that for the rest of my life."

My stomach was churning, but I held the tears at bay. I needed more. "Benjamin also said that when you learned the truth you did something to make sure it wouldn't happen to anyone again. I need proof of that before I can trust you. I want to believe you. I want you to be what you say, but—"

Clay nodded. "I'll get you that proof. I hear you, but I still think you should meet my friends. I've had time to think and I realized that to see who I am you need to meet the people who have helped me become a better person. On the surface the Barringtons look perfect, but they have suffered as well. Not the way you have, but in their own way. They have fought, doubted each other, and somehow always come back together. I failed you, Caterina, and there's nothing I can do about that. But I love you and I want you in my life. Please, come inside, bring a whole army if you need to, but give this a chance. We can figure it out. I have to believe that. We were all manipulated by our uncle. He can't win. I refuse to let evil like that win."

I looked over my shoulder at my friends who were standing quietly with several of Benjamin's security. Then I looked up at Benjamin.

He must have seen my question in my eyes because he gave my hand a squeeze and he said, "It's your decision, Caterina. We don't have to go in. You don't have to meet anyone. No one will force you do anything again. What do you want to do?"

The love in his expression gave me the ability to believe him. I turned back to my brother and put my fear aside. I didn't have to give him another chance. I could walk away and never see him again if I wanted to.

That wasn't what I wanted.

I wanted to believe his version and to find a way to be like the family he'd described. Was that kind of healing truly possible? I needed to believe it could be. "If we can all come inside, I'm willing to meet your—"

"Friends," Benjamin supplied.

"Yes." If Clay had found people who cared for him I didn't begrudge him that, but I wasn't ready yet to call them what he and I didn't yet feel like.

So we went inside. All of us. Me, Benjamin, my friends, and eight of Benjamin's security. It was almost comically odd, but also somehow felt right.

Clay led us to a room off the foyer where a good number of people were gathered. The first two to approach were an older couple. There was nothing intimidating about the kind-looking woman or the dignified man at her side.

"Hello," the woman said with a warm smile. "My name is Sophie Barrington. It is such a pleasure to finally meet a member of Clay's family. I hope you don't mind that I brought my whole clan with me. Generations of them, some better behaved than others."

A laughing child ran past as she said that with a set of slightly younger twins in hot pursuit. "It's nice to meet you. I brought a few people myself."

As if there was nothing unusual about someone showing up with so much security, the man next to her said, "I'm this wonderful woman's husband, Dale Barrington. You could say that I'm at least half responsible for all the chaos you'll witness here today. I suppose if we wanted quiet we shouldn't have had seven children. No complaints, though. We've unofficially adopted a few as well so we must be gluttons for punishment."

"Like my brother?"

"Like your brother," Sophie said gently. "I don't know what kept you out of each other's lives, but I do know what it's like to have a second chance with someone you didn't think you ever could. Clay has always seemed like he was searching for something that we couldn't be for him. I see now that it was you. I hope the two of you work things out and just know that we are here for you in any way that you might need us to be."

It was almost too much—too kind for me to handle in a first meeting so I didn't have a response to it. Benjamin stood at my side, hand on my back and introduced himself. Sophie and Dale moved on to introduce themselves to my friends as well as the men with them. Benjamin and I walked with Clay and Lexi farther into the room. He introduced us to so many people I couldn't remember their names, but what mattered was the pattern I saw emerging. One by one they seemed to be genuinely happy to meet us, and all of them seemed to care about Clay. There were movie stars, businessmen, artists, and one very scary looking man with several scars on his face.

Clay asked us to step off to one side of the room when he introduced us to him. "Caterina, this is Bradford and Ian." Clay lowered his voice. "Benjamin, these are the mechanics I spoke to you about."

Benjamin shook their hands. "To put some of our concerns at ease, do either of you have any proof that the problems with the vehicle have been resolved?"

The scarred man, Bradford, bent his head toward me and asked, "What kind of proof would reassure you? I'd prefer not to, but I can bring you whatever you need."

I swallowed hard. "I just need to know that they won't

hurt anyone else."

He bent lower and growled. "I made sure of it myself."

In a smooth tone, Ian added, "These kinds of conversations are best had in private. I understand though that I could never understand how you feel. We work for the government, but Bradford and I still take on side projects now and then. The less proof we retain the better it is for all of us. Careful what you ask for, though. There are things you can't unsee."

I realized then that I didn't want the weight of more details. "I don't want that either."

Bradford leaned in again. "I have to live with what I do, but it's easier than living with knowing that they're out there doing what they did to you to anyone else. I took care of your problem for you, for those they had, for those they would take, and to honor the memory of my sister. You are safe, Caterina Landon. And I'll make sure you always are."

Benjamin let out an audible breath. "That's—"

I stepped forward and gave Bradford a tight hug. In his eyes I had seen a pain that mirrored or surpassed my own and suddenly his scars were beautiful. He didn't hug me back, but he didn't need to. He'd already done more for me than I could ever express gratitude for. And it had cost him in a way I understood. He chose to carry that weight for me. "Thank you, Bradford."

When I stepped back, Benjamin put an arm around me. "You okay?"

I met Bradford's gaze. "No, but I'm not scared anymore."

Bradford nodded and walked away. Ian went with him.

I turned to Clay. "You didn't know."

His lips thinned to a straight line. "I didn't. I hate myself for not doing more, for missing the signs. For putting how I felt first."

I reached out and touched his arm lightly. "If I continue to hate myself and you hate yourself then our uncle really does win, doesn't he? He wanted to take everything from us and he did." I leaned into Benjamin's side. "But we can take it back. I found someone who loves me for who I am. I hope you have that with Lexi."

He hugged his wife closer. "I do."

I looked around the room to where Lorraine, Keiona, and Emmie were happily mingling with the Barrington clan. "I found friends who feel like family. And so have you."

"Yes."

I sniffed. "All that's left is to forgive each other and ourselves."

He held out a hand to me. "I want that—so much."

I searched his face without taking his hand. "Do you really think we could be a family again?"

"I do," Clay said in a gravelly voice. "The Barringtons have taught me a lot about loyalty and forgiveness. I'm sure it won't be perfect at first, but if we both want it we'll figure it out."

Benjamin gave the side of my head a kiss and it sent a burst of light through me. I looked at Lexi and decided to take ownership of my own journey. "Lexi, I never had a sister, but I'd like to try to be one to you."

Lexi flapped her hands in the air. "Willa is better at this emotional stuff than I am, but be warned that I'm a twin, so you technically just got yourself two sisters. Can I hug you?"

I smile. "Of course."

There was a lot of healing for me in that hug. I wasn't ready yet to hug Clay, but I could now imagine a day when I would be. He seemed to understand.

"Benjamin," Clay said. "I'll accept your donation to the Landon Foundation now."

"You bet your ass you will," Benjamin said without missing a beat.

I hid a smile behind my hand. Clay might intimidate some, but not my man.

A few minutes later, Benjamin bent near my ear and said, "Your friends seem to be holding up okay."

I sought them out in the crowd and was relieved to see he was right. Lorraine and Keiona were laughing with a small circle of Barringtons. Emmie had ditched the security for a conversation with two incredibly tall, buff movie stars. It didn't matter to her that their wives were at their sides or to the wives that she was a little smitten with their men. "She cracks me up. I've been out with her and her husband and he doesn't care. You'd think he'd be jealous, but he just laughs with her."

"He knows she loves him and that's all that matters."

I looked up at Benjamin. "I wouldn't have been brave enough to come here if it weren't for you."

"Yes, you would have. Remember how we met? You were strong then, you're strong now. I'm just your backup."

"And I'll always be yours."

He smiled and kissed my forehead. "Good because my parents are really bugging me to bring you over to see them. They don't know your secret and they don't ever have to, but they will grill you on if you want children, how many you want, and if they should have a swing set installed in their backyard now or later. They're that bad and that excited that I'm going to ask you to marry me."

My mouth fell open. "You—you—"

"Not now. Not here. I'm just planting the seed so you have time to get used to the idea."

I didn't know what to say to that so I just stood there with my mouth hanging open. Kids ran circles around us. Laughter erupted from the group Emmie was talking with. I met Clay's eyes across the room and smiled. Without taking time to second-guess myself I said, "I'm ready to see your parents and I'm ready for that proposal when you want to ask me."

I glanced up at Benjamin. His answer was a kiss that took my breath away.

Chapter Twenty-Three

Benjamin

LATER THAT EVENING, I sat on the couch at my apartment with Caterina snuggled on my lap. Mentally and physically exhausted, I could only imagine how she felt. I couldn't remember the last time I'd had so much adrenaline pumping for as long as I'd had that day. The fear I'd felt for her could have only been a hint of the fear she'd faced. She might not see it, but she was braver than most of the people I knew.

I glanced at Tasha's memorial box. Like you.

I understand now why you needed to fight for what you believed in. Had things turned out differently, I would have given my life for Caterina without hesitation. I would have done it because I love her, but you died saving strangers. There must be a special place in heaven for heroes like you.

I thought about the people Clay had surrounded himself with. I know I already have you working overtime keeping Caterina safe, but there's someone else I'd like you to watch over. I don't know what his story is and, God knows, I don't want to know what he has seen and done, but if anyone tries to lock that man out of heaven, open a damn window and let him in. He did what I couldn't have done myself and I know that cost him."

Caterina moved against my chest and I smiled down at her. I'm going to ask her to marry me. Yes, she knows. I know, I didn't choose the best time or place to tell her my plans, but you know I've never been good at expressing myself. "Give a man credit for trying."

Caterina raised her head. "What did you say?"

I kissed her lips gently. "Sorry, talking to Tasha—" I stopped there, hoping it wouldn't upset Caterina that I was sitting there thinking of my past wife.

"Does she answer you?"

"No, but I'd like to think she can hear me. I didn't understand her when she was here and I'd like to think it brings her comfort to know that I do now."

"A Marine. How do you go from a strong woman like that to . . . me?"

I took a moment to choose my words. "If you could see yourself through my eyes you'd never talk about yourself that way. When I look at you all I see is a strong survivor, someone who never gave up, never let the bad in life beat her. Tasha would have talked to you once and recognized that. I know I did."

With a smile, Caterina asked, "If I'm so brave why does the idea of dinner with your parents scare me?"

"Oh, you should be afraid. Very afraid. My mother is probably working on learning a new recipe to cook just for you. And don't tell her I said it, but she's awful in the kitchen. My mother could make toast taste terrible."

Caterina laughed. "She can't be that bad."

"Trust me, if the food is delicious it'll mean that her recipe failed and she had our cook throw something together."

"I'm a decent cook."

I tucked some of her hair back from her face. "I'm not with you for your culinary skills."

A smile spread across her face and she wiggled her beautiful ass against my hardening cock. "I wonder what skills I could possibly have that you might be with me for."

Running a hand up and down one of her thighs, I said, "You are quite good at all things related to that, but that's also not why I'm with you."

She stilled and her expression turned serious.

I answered the question in her eyes. "I like who I am when I'm with you. I'm not perfect and I'll probably do a good share of things I'll need to apologize for, but I'd given up on ever being happy again. I didn't think I could be. I'm not a different man. I don't believe people can really change who they are. But you helped me look inward and start living again."

She ran a hand lightly over my cheek. "I like who I am when I'm with you too. I used to want to be anyone but me, but I don't hate the person I see in the mirror anymore. Sometimes she disappointments me, but overall she's doing better . . . much better." She tipped her head to one side. "Thank you for everything you did today. Thank you for standing by me, letting it be my choice, and for understanding that I needed my friends as well."

I sat up straighter at that. "You're a genius!"

"I am?"

"Let's invite your friends to the dinner with my parents."

"We can do that?"

I felt suddenly freer. "My mother would love your friends and they would give us the buffer I'd like. Have them bring their husbands. My mother loves dinner parties. I'll ask Martina to join us. I heard she's dating a chef now so my mother will definitely use her house cook. It could actually be fun."

Caterina turned so she was facing me, straddling my lap. "Do you have any idea how much I love you?"

I wiggled my eyebrows. "I believe so, but perhaps you should show me just to make sure."

So I did. More than once. And then again in the morning because her touch was so tender, so loving it was a healing pleasure.

Chapter Twenty-Four

Benjamin

TWO WEEKS LATER Caterina and I were seated at a long, formal table at my parents' house. In all we were seven couples. My parents, Caterina's friends along with their husbands, Martina and her chef friend, Clay and Lexi, and us. We'd put Clay right next to my parents because . . . well, he deserved it. All my parents knew about their relationship was that they were coming out of a bit of a rocky patch.

My mother leaned toward him and said, "So, do you two have any little ones?"

"Not yet," Lexi said lightly. "My sister is doing her share to over-populate the planet, though, so we're in no rush."

My mother shook her head. "You really shouldn't wait, long before you wrinkle on the outside you're shriveling up on the inside."

"Speak for yourself," Keiona chimed in. "Lexi, you have plenty of time."

Emmie added, "Actually, female fertility peaks for a woman in her late twenties. It's all downhill after that. By age forty-five most women can't conceive without medical assistance. Fun fact, though, a woman's sexual prime actually occurs later in life. Women in their forties and later often have a higher sex drive. Don't you agree, Margaret?" Emmie leaned over and elbowed my father's ribs. "I hope for your sake she does."

I choked on a laugh at the shocked expression on my mother's face. My father barked out a laugh. Caterina covered her mouth with her hand, but her eyes were brimming with humor.

My mother took my father's hand in hers and with a straight face said, "Women are like wine, we get better with age." Then she winked at Emmie and there was more laughter around the table.

Once the group settled, my father said, "We're just glad Benjamin found someone while we're still young enough to enjoy our grandchildren. Clay, imagine how wonderful it would be if your children were able to grow up with Caterina's. Cousins are such a wonderful thing to have. Margaret and I were both only children so Benjamin was brought up alone. Looking back, I wish we'd had more, but Benjamin can make it up to us by filling our house with little ones."

"Filling it?" Caterina asked with wide eyes.

"We're not quite at that stage yet, Dad." As any good sibling would, I decided a little deflection was in order. "Martina might be, though. Martina, can we expect an announcement from you any time soon?"

A yelp from Lorraine's husband meant that the kick she'd directed my way had landed left of me. "Oh, my God," Martina said. "I'm sorry, Ted. I must have had a leg spasm."

Leaning down to rub his leg, Ted said, "Warn me the next time you feel a spasm coming on and I'll move so your target isn't blocked."

Caterina turned to me and lowered her voice so only I could hear. "It's going better than I thought it would."

I nodded and leaned to whisper in her ear. "Would you be okay if I asked you here?"

She turned to meet my eyes. "Right here?"

"Unless you want me to wait."

She looked around the table then back at me. "Actually, now would be kind of perfect."

I rose to my feet and cleared my throat. All eyes turned to me. "I am so glad all of you were able to come today because I have something I've been wanting to ask Caterina and it'll be even better with all of you here."

My mother and father could not have been smiling more.

Clay and Lexi held hands while they watched.

Martina and her girlfriend got all goofy happy.

Caterina's friends fell silent in anticipation.

I went down onto one knee and took out a ring box I'd been carrying around for the past two weeks. "Caterina Landon, loving you was something I didn't expect and something I am grateful for beyond what I know how to express. You brought me back to life. Will you marry me and allow me to spend the rest of my life as your partner in love, crime, parenting, or whatever else life throws our way? I can't imagine my life without you in it, so take that into consideration as you make your decision."

"There's no decision to make," Caterina said, "I'm all in. I want to make this legal, make those babies, and bring our children to visit our friends at the cranberry bog every year. You are the single best thing that has ever happened to me and if you think you could leave here without putting that ring on my finger you'd have to think again. So, yes, Ben. Yes. Yes. A hundred yeses."

"Does this count as another one for me?" Clay asked.

"No, hon," his wife answered. "But it's still wonderful."

Benjamin slipped the ring on my finger and rose to his feet. I stood as well and we kissed as our friends and family clapped.

"I knew it," my mother said. "And I couldn't be happier."

Practically hopping with excitement, I made my way around the table showing people the ring and hugging them. When I got to Clay he rose to his feet and I wrapped my arms around him. "I'm glad you were here for this."

His eyes welled up. "Me too." Then he shook Benjamin's hand and said, "I want an invite to that wedding as well."

"Invite?" Caterina hugged Lexi then turned to Clay. "You're the one I'd want to walk me down the aisle."

That was it. Clay lost it right there. Tears started rolling down his cheeks to the point where he excused himself for a moment.

"I didn't mean to upset him," Caterina said.

Lexi shook her head. "You didn't. You did the opposite. He loves you so much. You have no idea how much what you just said meant to him."

Clay returned looking more composed. "I would love to give you away."

Caterina took both of his hands in hers. "You'll be walking me, not giving me away. I'm not going anywhere. Not ever again."

I almost lost it then, but I held it together.

When we were all settled back at the table, the conversation turned to other subjects and there was an easy camaraderie that I took as a good omen. Caterina and I had turned a corner. Life would still throw challenges at us, but we would be able to handle them because we had each other.

As we were parting at the end of the night, Clay and Lexi took Caterina and me aside for a moment. "I know you don't know me well enough to know how good I am at things like this, but I'd like to plan your wedding for you. I'm really good at it. They don't call me a Fairy Godfather Extraordinaire for nothing."

Lexi said, "Oh, Clay, Caterina might have her own ideas about her big day."

Caterina took his hands in hers again and said, "I'll let you help me with the wedding if you help me with something else."

"Anything," he promised.

"Help me find Cooper and, if he's in rough shape, help me show him that no matter how he feels, our uncle didn't take everything away from him. He still has us."

I did shed a tear at that. Just one and I wiped it away before anyone noticed. Loving a Landon was a fucking emotional roller-coaster ride, but one I never wanted to end.

Clay sniffed and nodded. "I'll have Bradford track him down."

"Bradford?" The question burst out of me.

Clay dismissed my concern with a wave. "He also does nice things."

Caterina turned, wrapped her arms around me, and said, "We're getting married."

I kissed her forehead. "That's what I hear."

"Should I ask Martina if she'll be a bridesmaid? You know, just so you can torture her with really frilly dresses?"

A huge smile spread across my face. "You would do that for me?"

"I've got your back," she said with a laugh and I fell even harder for her.

Now that is a partner.

The End

Fresh Cranberry-Orange Cookie Recipe

A gift from my family to yours.

I'd love to hear from you about how you liked or modified the recipe.

rcardello@ruthcardello.com

If you include a photo I just might contact you and send you a little surprise.

Ingredients:

Cranberries (at least a cup)

Egg (1)

Butter (3/4 cup, softened)

Salt (½ tsp)

Vanilla (1 tsp)

Brown Sugar (1 cup)

Granulated white sugar (1/2 cup)

Baking powder (¼ tsp)

Baking soda (½ tsp)

Flour (2 ½ cups)

Orange juice (5 tbsp.) (*use in both the cookies and the glaze*)

Powdered Sugar (1 ½ cups) (*for the glaze*)

Orange zest (1 tsp) (*for the glaze*)

Directions:

1. Heat oven to 350 degrees.

2. In a large bowl cream butter and sugars (*brown and granulated, not powdered. Save the powdered for your glaze*) together until light and fluffy. Mix in vanilla and egg then 2 tbsp. orange juice and 1 tbsp. of orange zest.

3. In another bowl, combine the flour, baking soda, baking powder and salt then add to sugar mixture. Mix in the fresh cranberries. You can also use dried ones.

4. Drop large, rounded tablespoons of the dough onto cookie trays lined with parchment paper.

5. Bake for 8-10 minutes. Don't let them overbrown. They will harden as they cool.

6. Let cool while preparing cookie glaze.

7. In a small bowl stir together: 1 tsp of orange zest, 1 ½ cups powdered sugar, and 3 tbsp. orange juice. Mix until it forms a thin glaze. Then drizzle on cooled cookies.

Ways to switch it up:

*   Add white chocolate chips
*   Add nuts (pecans are a common choice)
*   Use shortening instead of butter
*   Use cranberries instead of raisins in your favorite oatmeal cookie recipe (or add one cup of uncooked quick oats)
*   Replace half of the butter with applesauce for a healthier treat
*   Replace the glaze with a dip into dark chocolate (melt with tsp of butter)

Decorate the plate of cookies with sugared fresh cranberries.

1 bag of fresh cranberries + 2 cups of sugar.

1. Dissolve ½ cup of sugar into ½ cup of water in a saucepan over medium heat.
2. Stir in cranberries until coated. Scoop with a draining utensil and let sit for at least an hour. Take the remaining 1 ½ cup of sugar and place it on an area you'll be able to roll the cranberries through the sugar with.
3. When the cranberries are well coated with sugar let them dry again then place in a small bowl beside your batch of cookies or sprinkle them around the cookies on a display tray.

Printed in Great Britain
by Amazon